Gateways to Abomination

Matthew M. Bartlett

ISBN: 1500346721
ISBN-13: 978-1500346720

For all who listened...

Contents

Gateways to Abomination

Don't startle or scare. Disturb. Upset. Remove the floor and dissolve the walls.
 -Abrecan Geist, Sinister Mechanisms *p. 45*

There are four separate and distinct methods by which one may disinter and defile the hardened heart.
 -Abrecan Geist, Sinister Mechanisms *p.106*

the woods in fall

are stark and open, the twisted trunks and gnarled branches standing out black against the gray wall of the sky.

The woods in spring and summer twitch and writhe with twittering birds and thick green life, even at dusk.

But in Fall the woods are foreboding and defiant. The brambles and bristles and thorns gather to hinder your progress, as though guarding a secret. As you pick your path and make your way through the trees, the day turns to night only yards in. In Fall, in the New England woods, it is always night. Leaves fall like dry, dead angels, piling up against the leviathan broken bones of storm-savaged trees.

It was Fall when I went into the woods. I had been in the den, sorting through papers with the radio tuned to classical music from a local college. The cat jumped up on the telephone table and ran his tooth along the side of the radio, turning the dial a few notches to the left in the process. GodDAMMIT, I said, sitting up to re-adjust the radio.

I stopped, my hand poised over the dial. I listened. And then I took up my stick and walked out of my house. I turned onto Allyn Street. The traffic whooshed by, and the freezing rain struck my face like needles. I felt the ice bouncing off of my eyeballs. A Stop & Shop bag fluttered desperately in a tree like a trapped ghost. I went into the woods.

I couldn't hear the road anymore when I saw the thin man. He was dressed in an old-style suit and a tall hat. I thought he might be distressed, but he moved through the uneven forest floor elegantly, as though strolling on a rain-slicked street.

When he got almost near enough for me to see his features, he bent suddenly, then dropped to his knees. His body whipped as though his spine were a snake snapped by a forceful hand. An ungodly gurgle bellowed up from his throat and he vomited a thick stream of wriggling worms. His body lurched again and he gagged, a thick crack, then drew in breath and let loose again, the worms pouring out as though propelled. I watched the folds of skin at his throat undulate. Then he took in a deep, retching breath and fell to the forest floor.

I rushed to him, my disgust giving way to pity and fear. When I got there, he looked dead, melted into the forest floor, reminding me of those pictures of soldiers' bodies engulfed in sand dunes at Normandy. His clothing twitched and writhed, and it was then I saw that the legions of worms had grown into snakes, with dripping fangs and black eyes. I smelled a sickly smell, of putrefaction and ammonia and venom. A wormy snake slid over my shoe, leaving a trail of black-green slime.

I fled the woods and the remains of the old man. Now I sit in my house. The power is out, and a fallen tree lets the rain into this dark den. It puddles at my feet. The cat floats by, its open eyes milky with cataracts, its body limp. The phone rings for a time, and then stops.

The door opens. I am not expecting anyone.

when i was a boy – a broadcast

When I was a boy in Leeds, I had a friend named Christopher Dempsey who lived out on Cemetery Hollow Road. He had a younger brother named Alex and a backyard that emptied out into an expanse of woods that hid most of our boyhood exploits, which for a time were no less innocent than catching and eating frogs.

Christopher and Alex each seemed to be clothed in dirt. It smudged their faces at the corners of their mouths and settled into the cracked skin at their elbows and knees. Their toes were so encased in filth they were never once kicked out of King's Grocery for being shoeless; a glance at their filthy feet fooled most into thinking the boys had donned dense and dirty slippers.

Their mother, though not as obviously caked and clotted with filth as her boys, seemed to be filthy with secrets. She was thick-hipped and black-haired and wore huge glasses and colorful faded sashes tied at her waist. She favored dark denim pantsuits and she smoked up hand-rolled cigarettes one after the other. She was ugly and beautiful and fat and curved and she did not wear lipstick neatly like Mother wore lipstick. She spent hours behind the closed door of her room listening to monotonous and eerie orchestral music.

She read strange books. She was quiet and sullen and cursed at her boys and humiliated and hated them. She took to me instantly, foisting her boys off upon me on many a hot afternoon and staring strangely after me as we fled into the woods.

I neither liked nor disliked Christopher and Alex. They were dim and easy to manipulate. Crimes I wished to commit they'd do at the mere suggestion. We committed acts of minor arson, and were cruel to frogs and otters and lizards, but not to cats. I once saw Christopher trying to strangle a tomcat and I jammed a thick branch into his ear until it spat blood and I handily convinced Alex to take the blame.

Before long, I became fixated on their mother. Her body was magnificent. Her ass was huge and hypnotic and I wanted to see all of it. The only naked images of women I'd seen were from drawings by my neighbor (and friend) Guy, and the lonely woman who lived next door and changed with the blinds not drawn. Guy had a talent for drawing wide, angular asses, and hers was like one he'd never dared draw, nor even imagine. I wanted to nestle in it like a cat in the crook of a tree. I wanted to inhale its mysterious dank odors. I wanted to sup at it, to beat at it with my balled fists, to set it on fire and burn myself putting it out, to roll in the ashes in leaves of burnt flesh like it was catnip in satin sheets. But I was but ten, and she had a long line of miserable unworthy suitors to tend to her musty desires.

Christopher and Alex and I would play hide and go seek in the yard and I would sneak to the bedroom window to see her, face down on the couch while some boney, scaly drunk's bone-white tiny ass whipsawed up and down. Hours later in my own bed I would hear all the sounds, the voices and the sounds of flesh and I would ejaculate into my cupped hand, my mouth wrenched open in horror and revulsion and ecstatic erotic joy.

Over the months of summer I saw the teacher Mr. Craston kicking rocks in her driveway, I saw some of the lean, hoodlum neighborhood kids smoking sullenly on her porch, and once I swore I saw my father emerge shamefully from her house and slink off behind their garage, but it couldn't have been. He was at work. But there were more, many of them, scores of them.

One day I arrived at their old house to find Alex and Christopher lashed to a tree in the back with a length of rope encrusted with something greenish brown. Christopher was howling, straining against the ropes, his fists balled, blood seeping from between his fingers and a swinging pendulum of brown drool clinging to his bruised and chapped bottom lip. Alex was opposite him, fast asleep, the corner of his tongue poking from his mouth like a swollen worm, a metronomic rasp the only sign of life. I noted that his shirt was yanked up where the rope pushed into his flesh and his little belly lolled. I noted that he had an outie.

I turned to leave and She beckoned me from the doorway. She was wearing a ratty pink robe that hung open obscenely. Its browned sash curled like a snake at her feet. I seem to remember--though it cannot be--that a newly lit cigarette jutted from between her disturbingly large big toe and its curled neighbor, sending a seductive tendril of smoke up past the webbed blue veins of her thighs, past the sweaty cramped horizons of her belly, past the glitter stuck in clumps between her ample, dangling breasts, past her eyes, one of which twitched, past her hair, which was greasy and brown and frayed. I turned again to run and fainted dead away.

I cannot describe what was happening to me when I woke. It was my dream come true and my nightmare. Her face pushed into me everywhere. She pulled from me pleasures I'd never imagined and pulled and bit at my skin angrily until I shrieked and pulled away in pain and shame. Cigarettes lay broken and smoking in ashtrays all over the room. There must have been scores of them, providing ample light to see the faces watching us from all the corners of the room. I thought I saw Guy grappling with my father over scraps of raw meat. I remember a clock whose face was an obscene caricature of a black man, another whose hands were crudely rendered pricks. I remember a dog rolling on a milk-soaked carpet, its belly a mass of grotesque breasts. She saw me looking frantically about the room and covered my eyes with her hand, which smelled of sex and nicotine.

There was music playing, I remember, and there were whispers and bursts of jeering laughter. I think at one point a dog lapped at the bottom of my foot. I endured a cigarette burn whose ghost still haunts my eyebrow. I remember the sounds of someone vomiting. But mostly there was her, from every angle and in deep in every fold. Our bodies roiled and boiled and pushed into each other unspeakably. I was terrified of her, and terrified that it would end. I was sure I would die, for there were long stretches of time when her flesh filled my throat and seemed to be on the verge of somehow invading my very lungs. I wanted to die, and I wanted to go on forever.

But I did not die, and I did not go on forever. After innumerable hours--days?--I was pushed naked into a shower and held against the wall so I wouldn't collapse. I was washed my many rough hands. I was fed stale bread and thin soup. After, I staggered out onto the lawn, drunk (for at one point she had spat vodka down my throat and slapped my face with a massive slipper). I collapsed, inhaling the smell of grass and healthy dirt. I was in love and in pain

8

and in lust and I was ashamed.

That night I burned down the house with kerosene and rags and father's whisky bottles. All the Dempseys died that night. Mr. Craston must have been there, because he never came back to school. The firemen and investigators swarmed the sooty, scorched mess for days after. I heard rumors of their findings, things in the basement, carcasses and cocoons and collections of obscene antiquities and rusty metal sexual apparatus that could not have been designed for humans. There were sixteen bodies found, but no one save Mr. Craston missing from our town. Old pages and parts of books in unfathomable languages. I saw them drag out the belt I'd worn during my hellish visit. I saw three-eyed spectacles and a bucket full of feet. Maybe I didn't see these things.

Maybe I dreamed them, or maybe I'm misremembering them.

Every woman after was but a shadow of her. I scared them all away anyway, what with my screams and my mutterings and my cruel and impossible demands. She was my First and my Last. She was a gateway to abomination.

You're listening to WXXT. You are not sure how long you have been listening. Your stomach drowns out the sounds of your radio. A wind howls. The batteries die. Infants mewl at your feet.

Up next, the swinging sounds of Dino Paul Crocetti. You know him as Dean Martin.

path

Bill, with one tightening hand, his left and weaker hand, held both of Elise's wrists together over her head. His right forearm strained toward the floor, her slender neck blocking it from its destination. He curled his hand into a fist and pushed his elbow down as if trying to close a paper cutter onto a ream of heavy stock.

He pushed harder, and her legs kicked and her midsection bucked. He closed his eyes, squeezing with one hand, leaning with the other.

He had never ridden a bull, not the flesh and fur kind, not the beer and bar and barrel kind, but he imagined this was what it was like: to stay on, to persevere, to make the noise stop…and finally the struggle ceased. He pushed further, using every last bit of energy, and heard a terrible noise. The death rattle? The room filled with a horrible smell, ordure, urine, animal smells, coffee breath.

The enormity hit him and he fell backwards, his taut legs propped up by her dead legs, his arms thrown back, his jaw open wide, scary wide, like a tin can with a whisker for a hinge. He heard an airplane overhead somewhere.

Why had she said that to him? In a blast of reflection he realized she couldn't have meant it; she was simply asserting the fact that she held authority, not actually threatening to use it.

There would be time to think about that later. He let his mind flood with the facts of this woman, her life. She had friends, people she wrote to. An ex-husband, a kid somewhere in a city miles away, but who saw her for holidays. Accounts at social networking sites. Thoughts about the future.

He let all that wash over him, and then he let it go.

In times of great stress, he would sometimes picture himself as an other, watching from somewhere else, calmly assessing, allowing himself to be entertained, even amused by what was happening to his lesser self. He was never so dramatic as to name this Other, never so self-deceptive as to think of it as alien or beast. It was just Bill, a Bill devoid of emotion, looking upon a scene as though it was happening in some depressing movie. Dispassionate. Detached.

In this manner Bill's other, and then Bill in turn, began to think of this problem not as a living, breathing human problem, but as a logistical problem, a puzzle, to be solved. He imagined he would be caught, publicized, humiliated, and punished. But he allowed himself a glimmer of hope, that this problem might do nothing more than cause many nights of self-torture. A self-imposed prison that still had cable and restaurants and streets.

Bill dragged the body into the bathroom and turned on the lights on either side of the mirror and the overhead light. He stepped into the kitchen and pulled a sharp blade from a drawer piled to the top with knives. He remembered only having only a few knives, and was momentarily puzzled. It threw him, actually, and he paused.

He shook it off.

Knowing from television that forensic investigators can find with special lights where blood has been spilled, Bill pulled Elise's body up so that she was draped over the toilet, her head lolling over the side. With his left hand he gripped her hair and with his right he pushed the blade of the knife into the delicate hollow of her throat. He pushed and twisted and gouged, expecting a torrent, a splashing, something. He heard only a trickle. He pulled the body to the side and saw only a dissolving spiral of blood, a deep red corkscrew fading to pink and hanging in the water like a ghost.

He felt a sudden and intense and specific physical shift in his guts and flung Elise to the floor. Her arm stuck up in the air awkwardly. He saw that at some point she'd scraped her elbow, saw the glimmering of her wedding ring. He shoved down his pants and sat and released, his head thrown back, his jaw taut.

13

After cleaning up and showering--he tried to avoid looking at the body through the haze of the translucent shower curtain liner--he stood over her, naked, drying himself with haste, feeling vulnerable and exhausted.

Somewhere in the house, a voice spoke.

Bill let out a shrill shriek and instinctively grabbed a towel and wrapped it over his midsection. His breath came in rasps, and he put his hand over his mouth and listened carefully.

The voice droned from somewhere in the house, and Bill heard soft music--it was the clock radio. He must have set the alarm, forgetting it was the weekend. Was it that late? He walked through the dark house cautiously, his collected furniture and books seeming to loom and threaten, the voice in the bedroom growing louder and more strident. He reached his shadowed bedroom, lit only by a reading lamp in the corner whose face was pushed to the wall to minimize glare.

The Plague of the Leech, an insistent and insinuating voice bleated from the tinny speaker, *will start in the stomachs of your children. The schools will close. Schoolteachers will fall in the street and men will lean to help and be taken. Hospitals will be overwhelmed and overrun; they will host the Leech and the Leech will simmer in its tubes and conduits and its tanks...*

The red lights showed not 6 a.m., the time he would

wake for work, but 3:17; Bill's vision suddenly doubled, creating a dim, ghostly 3:17 below the real one. He shook his head and it was still there. He switched the radio off, but the voice continued. Then he saw that, in fact, the clock radio sat precariously upon another clock radio.

The disease will roil in your stomachs and minds and your churches will burst like bellies of brick and glass... The voice rose in pitch and the music, an orchestral drone, deepened. Bill shoved the top radio aside and turned off its twin. Will this be the nature of my torture, he wondered.

He tried to separate from himself, look at the situation coldly from elsewhere, but he could not pull himself away. Bill was stuck in this, stuck in himself, and he was certain that the voice would rant again of death and plagues in a mad chorus of stacked radios teetering madly upon his dresser. He was certain he would be caught, and for a moment he wanted to be caught, to confess in mad sobs, gripping the phone so hard the plastic would crack.

He fought panic.

And then he separated. Parting from the whimpering man in the small house on the small street, pushing himself up above the trees like a swimmer pushing to the surface of a lake, Other Bill knew that daylight would come soon and that he must act. Bill remembered a place, a shadowed path in the meadows, and a dense and vast wood where as a

15

teenage boy he'd once found a stash of rain-dampened, swollen pornographic magazines. He remembered their smell, and it somehow brought him comfort. The path must be narrow enough for his modest car. He would bury her deep in the ground and hope that was enough.

He walked out of his room, his emotions and senses at rest. In his head, he was already on the shadowed path. Behind him the bedroom began to glow red, and a deeper red, and a mad voice began to speak, and double, and triple, and multiply.

As Bill stood over the body, which now seemed to him impossibly small, he realized he possessed no carpet in which to wrap it, and neither the tools nor the nerve necessary to dismember it.

Again, his heart began racing. His breath jumped into his throat in bursts. He feared each burst might be the last, that he might die here, collapse onto the small body curled on the floor and be found with her in a grim embrace, two silent cadavers awkwardly entangled, slowly stiffening and melting into the linoleum under an undulating umbrella of flies...

...and then he clenched his fists and again rose through the ceiling, through the attic, into the blue-black sky. He watched from above as his body pulled the comforter from the guest-room couch, bumped the body on top of it, and rolled the whole thing up into a bulging tube. He watched as he used packing tape to roll and tighten the ends. He smiled patiently as he came to the end of the roll, tearing cardboard off with the last strip of tape, and then rummaged through the junk drawer, finally locating a new roll. "You're doing fine," he whispered down to himself, a smile in his voice. "This will all be over soon."

Once he had awkwardly shuttled the body to the back seat of the car, he descended down into himself, coughed wildly, and started the engine. The defogger seemed to take forever. He avoided looking in the rear view, and clicked on the radio for distraction. The news was on, something about a bank robbery done by old men in topcoats, and then the vertical red line slid from the middle of the FM band to the left, voices and music and static flickering by, until it nearly disappeared behind the left-hand border.

...was the DeJackal Sisters with "Loosen My Bowels," a booming, echoing voice intoned. *Baphomet and bath mats; ravens and rape kits, strychnine and spikenard--the Hour of the Leech continues. Through your system like needles, blackening and crushing your cells, reshaping your synapses, tartening your tongue and boiling your brain in its skull...*

Bill reached to switch off the radio; the dial was as hot as fire--he drew back his hand and stared at the blisters boiling on his finger and thumb.

17

As the voice continued its rant, across the dashboard a series of radio dials lit up, turning the interior of the car a sickly glowing green, and the voice zipped around his head like a trapped insect. He looked up and the roof of the car was teeming with black radio speakers, bulging along with the booming voice. They were crawling with spiders. One of the speakers burst, spraying blood and tissue onto the passenger seat. Radio dials lit up along the door panels, on the steering wheel. Bill covered his ears, squeezed shut his eyes, and screamed.

When he opened his eyes and lowered his hands, the cacophony had abated. A low drone came from the speakers and the radio dials, still glowing from all around him, pulsed softly with green light. The befouled passenger seat sizzled quietly as the gore ate away like acid at the fabric.

Bill could only push forward. He drove out onto the main road, which was now somehow crowded on both sides with trees, behind which the dark windows of the silent houses watched. The treetops met above the road, muting the bright light of a spectacularly starry night. He drove for a time on the road, absent from himself, lost in the drone and the driving, unthinking. Eventually he turned the car onto the long dirt road that led through the woods to the path...

...to find himself in a procession of cars. The clock said

4:24 a.m. Who were these people? Where were they going? He felt compelled to shut his headlights, and did. So did all the other drivers. The road darkened in front and behind, leaving only the green glow that lit all the cars' interiors. Peering ahead, and whipping his head around to look behind, all he could see in the cars were silhouettes.

Slowly the somber parade turned onto the path and bumped along the forest floor. Before long, the procession halted. Bill hoisted himself out of the car, hearing the other car doors open as he did so. He turned and opened the rear door, dragging the comforter to the leaf-strewn ground. He shut the door and heard the other doors shut. How many? He could not tell. He looked down the line, and saw an endless procession of haunted men, each standing over a blanket-bound bundle. The nearest man to him was round faced and expressionless, though the green lights revealed an incarnadine face, splotched and tear-soaked. Bill felt tears on his own face.

The men in the woods pulled shovels from the trunks of their cars and hoisted their burdens over their left shoulders. All of the radios came to life, filling the morning with the drums of a military march. Birds joined in, chirping high and multitudinous. They scuttled through the treetops in the hundreds of thousands, their wings like thunder, the treetops hissing at their passage.

The morning was coming, the deep blue above the trees lightening, shooting down dusty shafts of blue through the trees. The ground was thick with earthworms, the vegetation blossoming, exploding, filling in the gaps of the forest. Bill struggled forward with his burden; he sobbed, he gibbered, he wept. To his left and to his right, men shouldered their way past the trees and underbrush, lugging their burdens.

All the men wept.

Then the sound of crashing, splintering trees, of wailing sirens, and a squadron of police cars bouncing from all directions through the burgeoning underbrush, some getting caught in the brambles, or upended by trees bursting up through the forest floor, blue and red lights dancing in the trees. Bill felt as though he was spinning in a tornado of light and noise. The body slipped from his shoulder. He sailed up into the funnel. It began to rain. His burden lay below. The other men rose around him, spinning slowly into the sky into the rain. Up, up they went. Bill looked down and picked himself out of the crowd. He looked so small down there. The smell of carrion followed him, the smell of gunpowder, the smell of morning rain soaking the earth.

Then the worms rose, and the leeches. They followed the men into the morning, eating the rain, the leaves, the sky.

the ballad of ben stockton verse 1

When in the Spring of 2010, I moved from Woodburn, Oregon back to New England, from whence my family came, among the first of my many tasks was to locate a dentist.

My new job at a publishing company offered dental insurance, a benefit I'd not been afforded for five years. I had let my teeth go to an extravagant extent, having lived in what could be generously termed "reduced circumstances." Though I had dark dreams about periodontal disease, I was not a prodigious eater of sweets and sugars, so I did have some little hope of having gotten away with something.

I looked through the HMO's online list of participating dentists and looked for a name that I would find sonorous. I happened upon Dr. Francis Styrax. Perfect. A hell of a way to select a dentist, I know, but I tend to save things like research for academic matters. I had recently defended my thesis, entitled "Solipsism and Egoism in Satanic Cults" and was keen on keeping my nose out from between book pages for an amount of time that was yet to be determined.

My first appointment was early on a Monday morning before work. The office was in a small strip of medical buildings including an emergency clinic and a Planned

Parenthood. I signed in at the desk and filled out the appropriate paperwork. Then I flipped through an issue of *People* until I was called.

The hygienist was young and raven-haired, with dark, sculpted eyebrows. Her body was the very picture of the hourglass shape. Very attractive. Her name tag informed me before she could that her name was Angel. She executed a perfect cleaning, during which I stole frequent looks at the smooth, utterly unblemished white skin of her throat and breastbone. If she saw me, she didn't catch on, though her face bore an expression of bored bemusement.

After a time I was asked to rinse, and had the dubious pleasure of watching shards of tartar circle down the tiny circular sink. Watching them swirl down in eddies of blood stirred something in me, some memory, and I clenched my whole body in a panic. The hygienist mistook my agitations as squeamishness or dental anxiety, and allowed me a few moments to gather myself.

After the cleaning she put a heavy vest over my chest and had me bite down on a hard, plastic apparatus that dug into my gums. After some adjustments--I apparently have a narrow, high palate--the X-rays were done and she informed me the doctor would shortly be in.

Dr. Styrax entered the room glowering at a clipboard. He was a bulky man with a squarish face, topped by grey hair swept to the side and a forehead crowded with horizons of deep wrinkles. His eyes were kind and slightly haunted, the former being a quality one might hope for in a dentist. "There is a shadow I'm seeing in your X-ray that is causing me some concern," he said. "I'd like to refer you to an oral surgeon who will take a closer look."

"Could it be cancer?" I asked, and he chuckled darkly.

"The classic first question," he said. "Cancer is not what concerns me." He handed me a folded sheet of paper with a phone number and a name: Dr. Goldmast Lisle-Pearl.

Later that day I called the number and a diffident sounding receptionist with a flat affect insisted I come in right away. She gave me an address in Holyoke. I received supervisory permission to take the afternoon off, and took the bus south.

On the bus I realized that Dr. Styrax had not quite answered my question.

The building was a tall, narrow, dilapidated high-rise on a long, featureless street. Most of the other buildings appeared to be vacant manufacturing facilities, and I saw no cars. The building was of gray stone, and dirty and cracked blinds were drawn in all the windows. I entered through a heavy, windowless oak door into a checkered floor lobby. An elevator with rusted doors was to my left, a stairwell to my right.

I pressed the button for the elevator and heard a shrill, metallic shriek somewhere up above, and then what sounded like debris tumbling through the elevator shaft and down to some unknown depths below. The elevator doors shook and strained, and then they parted, leaving a gap of about three inches and then shuddering to a halt, one of them becoming comically crooked in the process. Peering in, I could see only thick steel wound wire.

I started up the stairs. As I turned at the first landing, I heard strange footsteps echoing down the stairwell. Boom-slap, boom-slap, boom-slap. At the next landing I looked up and saw a man dressed as a clown coming down, navigating the stairs with drunken deliberation. He looked like he'd been doused with a bucket of water, unnaturally red curls flattened to his forehead below an absurdly tiny hat. He wore a polka-dotted smock sopping with moisture. His makeup was smeared to the degree that I could not tell if he had started the day a happy clown or a sad clown.

He avoided my gaze as he passed, and I turned and had something of a shock: his back was porcupined with long metallic needles. They sprung from between his shoulder blades in a patternless proliferation. A crescent of needles frowned from his lower back. Below that, he was wearing a set of plastic buttocks, tied around his waist with a grey wet string. There was no blood that I could see.

My rationality has always been there for me. In arguments it has been my weapon; when the world has come growling at me with teeth bared, it has been my shield. I held onto it now. If Dr. Styrax had recommended an oral surgeon, I must be headed to see an oral surgeon. It is just that...my family, my background. There is a history of strangeness about which I don't want to speak. I can only say that I fled that strangeness as a boy of sixteen. I changed my last name, cut off all ties, moved across the country. My life has been the very picture of normalcy since then. So my guard was up, but so was my determination to look after my health. I continued.

As I rounded the next landing, a goat rounded the one a flight up, a stricken look on its narrow face. It clomped down the stairs at an awkward angle, back hooves left, front hooves right. It glanced at me guardedly and, I swear, groaned, and continued past. At the next landing I opened the heavy door and found myself in a nondescript hall that smelled of cedar and new paint. Wooden doors with frosted glass panels lined the hall. My folded page indicated 13-18. I read the stenciled lettering on the doors as I walked. 13-3 BARNET COLLEGE DEPARTMENT OF THEOSOPHIC STUDIES...13-12 DR. WHELAN GEIST FATES THERMAL AURICULAR THERAPY...

The door for 13-18 said DR. GOLDMAST LISLE-PEARL in letters worn and chipped, and then ORAL SURGEON in letters that shone black and new. I touched my finger to the "O" and the door swung open at my touch. I looked at my fingertip, and it was blue-black. The "O" on the door was smudged.

notice – 1802

WHEREAS Permilia, my wife, has for some time past behaved herself in a very unbecoming and threatening manner, abusing and ill-treating me--her lawful husband-- biting and scratching like a cat gone mad, without any just cause or provocation, and hath run me considerably in debt, and hath committed the crime of Adultery in the bed of AMASA MILKERTON with an excess of Eight Men, and has joined with the Amalekites in the Worship of the Leech, this is to forbid all persons from trusting her and harboring her on my account. I will pay not any bills of her contracting. Reward for her return in a mortal condition or for clews as to her whereabouts.

interview with emily lavallee-- september 2007

Q: What happened Tuesday night?

A: There was a frantic knocking at our door, late. My husband bolted up out of his chair and I told him, don't answer it. Call the police. He's so trusting. He was so trusting.

Subject cups face in hands.

Q: What happened next?

A: John opened the door. At first I thought it was...it looked like the creature from the Black Lagoon...scaly, or something, and wet...though it wasn't raining. It burst into the foyer, and there was a muffled screaming.

Q: Did it say anything? Could you make out any words?

A: No, just this muffled screaming. Then one of the scales detached itself. It was bloated...it was a leech. It looked like a frog's...you know, a frog's throat when it expands? It was purplish. Horrifying.

Q: What did it do when it detached?

A: It unfolded these wings, and then it tried to fly...there was this horrible, loud buzzing...then it hit the corner of the coffee table and kind of... (Long pause) It exploded. There was blood in my coffee cup...one of the wings was fluttering on top of a book...

Q: What was John doing at this point?

A: He was getting a lighter from the kitchen. He flicked it and put it on one of the things...on the man's face. I swear to you that the thing screamed. It screeched and then it...sort of undulated. Have you ever seen a cat throw up? It was like that, like someone was turning a lever...

Q: It was regurgitating into the wound.

A: Ugh. Ah.

Q: What happened next?

A: I just started pulling the things off, prying them up between their heads and their tails, sliding my hands back and forth. John did too. We cleared the man's neck, and part of his face. I think. I think he. I think he was dead. Those things were holding him up. They all started fluttering their wings. The ones we'd pried off were struggling to fly, or crawling around blindly.

Somewhere in there John must have called 911. The police came. They had no idea what was going on. John and I just got down on the floor and put our hands over our heads. They shot the man. He wouldn't fall. He just wouldn't fall.

Q: How do things stand now? What happened next?

A: We told the police everything they told you. An ambulance came, and then a pest control service. Slaughton's Pest Control, I think they were called. They declared the house uninhabitable until further notice, and the police contacted the Red Cross and got us a room at the Best Western by the highway. We were allowed to pack.

Q: And then?

Pause.

A: John was undressing to shower when he found it. He started screaming for me, and when I came in...It was like John was hanging in midair...face towards the ceiling. He was breathing in these...in jagged rasps. A leech had him, see? It was burrowed into his chest. It was huge...like a giant fat fly...its wings were a blur and it had him. John looked at me, but his eyes...he couldn't see me. His mouth opened and it was...it was like the sound of static, like bursts of static, and then some horrible laugh, and this voice. This dripping, venomous voice.

Q: What did the voice say?

A: It said, "It worked. It works. It has begun."

the ballad of ben stockton verse 2

I found myself in a smallish room illuminated only by small bulbs in display cases and in glass-fronted shelves that lined the walls to my left and my right. Opposite the door I had entered was another door with a stained glass window that afforded a little more light, though muted.

The case nearest to me contained an ancient looking box with wooden dials and metal switches. As I walked through the room, I saw that it was clearly the display-room of a collector of radios and radio technology.

In the middle of a room was a radio in a highboy cabinet; beyond that sat transistors; some colorful plastic, some gray; and tabletop radios; then a series of walkmen; and a blue and white MP3 player that presumably contained an FM receiver.

What was baffling, though, was the last two cases. They were large terrariums, one on either side of the door with the stained glass window.

The one on the left had a floor of pebbles in tones of rust and sandstone, and a path of jagged rectangular brick-red stones leading to a flat, hollowed-out rock that looked like a child's wading pool made of marble. A thick thatch of ferns provided a bright green backdrop, and wee potted plants dotted the ground. In the back corner sat an antique chair, no bigger than your thumb, painted in exquisite detail. On that chair sat a fat black fly involved in a process that looked much like grooming. As I watched, two more flies emerged from the lush backdrop and hovered at the glass. It appeared as though they were looking at me.

Unnerved, I stepped back and then started to cross to the other terrarium, when the door swung open to reveal what appeared to be a sparse waiting room. Not wanting to appear rude, I walked in.

The room was brightly lit, causing me to squint through my fingers. The walls were bright white. There were no pictures on the wall, just a window with white blinds drawn tight. Before me was a squarish, low coffee table on which sprawled a haphazard pile of *Newsweeks*, *Peoples*, and *Highlights for Children*. Catty-corner, framing the table on two sides, was a pair of mismatched cheap couches, one industrial brown, one off-white to the point of being dingy.

Ahead of me was a glassed-off receptionist area where a slender, redheaded girl sat. Her hair was tied into pigtails and she wore garish green eyeshadow. She scratched her eye and I saw that her left hand was without fingernails. Her eyebrows, it seemed, were nonexistent; instead two curved, thin arches were drawn on, one slightly higher than the other--by accident or design, I wondered. The left eyebrow was slightly smudged: I could see the whorl of a partial fingerprint. It reminded me of the lettering on the door.

"You can have a seat," she said.

"There's no paperwork for me to fill out?"

She sighed wearily, apparently irritated that her statement was threatening to transition into a conversation.

"No," she said conclusively, and turned to rifle noisily through a black file cabinet.

Before I could sit, the door next to the receptionist area opened, revealing a very tall, gaunt man with deep set eyes and hair of black and silver that sat flat on his head and draped down behind his neck, curling up at the ends in an almost feminine affect. He wore the beleaguered face of an addict, red-eyed and deep-wrinkled, his eyes shining from dark hollows.

"Mr. Stanton," he grinned, and I saw that his teeth were in shambles--browned, broken. I swore that I saw one tooth...a lateral incisor?...swinging from a sinuous pink thread from an expanse of red upper-gum. He wore a white jacket over a blue Arrow shirt, pressed khakis, and ostentatious cowboy boots whose toes ended in a narrow point. "I am Dr. Lisle-Pearl."

I was about to open my mouth to invent some kind of excuse to leave, when his enormous hand clapped my shoulder and steered me down a short hall and into a room in which loomed a dental chair and the attendant apparatus. They seemed too big for the room. On one wall was the obligatory painting of a flowered landscape; on another a browned poster displaying a potbellied cartoon of a man, meant to be Asian, in profile. A series of horizontal lines led from the body to an impenetrably tight, smushed series of Asian characters--that kind of lettering that always looked to me like intricate illustrations of impossible houses.

The doctor directed me to sit in the chair and told me pointedly to relax. Then in walked a hygienist with bulbous features too large for her small head. Her hair was pulled back so tightly that there were vertical lines on her forehead which, set against her natural lines, formed a painful looking crosshatch effect. Her name tag read "Sithyl" and her white coat was terribly tight and short, and it looked to me as though she might be wearing nothing under it. Her large (though muscular) legs were quite bare, and dark blue varicose veins pulsed at her ankles.

She was on me in an instant, reaching under the chair, her mountainous chest pushed up against my side. Her perfume was unbearable; it smelled of rotten fruit and incense. She pulled up a set of brown leather straps, clipping and locking the buckles over my forearms and stomach, then another over my ankles.

I started to protest and the doctor wheeled around and

jammed some kind of apparatus into my mouth. I only caught the merest glimpse over Sithyl's bulging shoulder, but it looked like some kind of multi-clawed, metallic insect with a body like an intricate drafting compass. It clamped onto my back teeth and then, as the doctor reached in and turned a dial, cranked open my mouth to the point I feared my muscles would tear. I tasted metal and my own blood.

Then the body of the thing seemed to expand, pushing down my tongue and up against the roof of my mouth. I tried to protest again, and a cold sensation lightly tapped the back of my palate, as though a small arm had extended, and activated my gag reflex. I said, "GEH."

"Try not to speak," the doctor said, grinning a benevolent grin under dead eyes. He opened a plastic door in the side of the chair and uncoiled a long corrugated tube with a curved triangular mask, which he fitted over my mouth and nose and then affixed with straps behind my head.

"Too tight?" he asked, and I was instinctively, appallingly grateful that when I nodded, he actually loosened the straps.

He flipped a switch and air pushed into my nose and throat. It smelled sweet, with a hint of almond. The music from the speakers in the ceiling, a barely noticeable Muzak, began to swell. An insistent cello rose up, accompanied by some kind of intense, whispered chanting. The hygienist put her chubby hand between my legs, staring lustily into my eyes. Against all my senses, I began to feel profound arousal as her hand began to undulate in a way that I would have thought physically impossible. It was as though she had fifty fingers. My jaw hung open. The doctor inserted a plastic tube that slurped out the saliva. My eyes filled with tears of gratitude and love.

Then he pulled out a tray table. On it was a pile of rusted, wood-handled dental implements, some simple and familiar, some alien and alarmingly complex, like an eight-tanged set of scissors with four rubber grips, and a smaller set of shears with one blade and one long antenna that appeared to have been torn from a car and inexpertly soldered to the other stub where a blade had once been.

The doctor grabbed a long tool with a circle of metal at one end. Suddenly his arms went all long and thin, like licorice. He plunged them into my mouth as Sithyl began some kind of new manipulation that caused my head to fall slowly back against the head-rest. At the ceiling, winged babies wheeled. Their wings were black gossamer and they gibbered with wet beaks of pink and purple. They had the eyes of goats. Their diapers bulged.

When finally I looked back down, four of my teeth were on the tray table in a pool of blood. On a small washcloth-- with a Comfort Inn logo--rested four new teeth. Two were of translucent glass. Of those, one contained what appeared to be a microscopic circuit board; the other a thin metal pole down the center.

The other two teeth were white on the sides, but on the top looked like radio speakers.

I looked back up to the ceiling. One of the babies was flitting against the ceiling tiles like a moth. A line of pink drool detached from its lower lip and lit across Dr. Lisle-Pearl's forehead.

Sithyl's hand quickened, and I felt myself release as though it had been years. Suddenly, shockingly, the doctor walloped her with a powerful backhand. She flew backward off of her stool and sprawled on the carpet, her mouth agape. I could now confirm that she wore nothing under her white coat.

I averted my gaze, which I let slide right past the terrifying infant. I looked at the doctor's impassive face. He grinned, his teeth a decrepit bone-yard. Then he held up the eight-bladed scissor, his arm went thin and he thrust it into my throat, deep, deep, impossibly deep. My lips ringed the doctor's white-coated elbow. I tasted fabric. I blacked out.

wxxt news brief

LEEDS, Mass. - There were new details Wednesday morning about why a Hampshire County school bus driver lost his job.

The school system fired Stanley Saltworth in May. According to Saltworth's personnel file, the former bus driver had numerous formal complaints lodged against him. He was terminated shortly afterward.

One parent said Saltworth wept while picking up students. Another said that he demanded a female middle school student check his back for leeches. Other parents complained he played at top volume on the bus a radio station that was broadcasting obscene material. Saltworth insisted that the bus radio was defective.

wanted dead

WANTED DEAD: Guy RONSTADT, in shape resembling a man, he stands about 19 1/2 hands high, with tangled Hair, a patrician Nose, engaging Eyes, and unseemly Ears. Turn a deaf ear to his persuasions, as he has acquaintance with neither Truth nor Decency. He has more Devil in him than Rasputin ever had. He is a thief and a murderer and a defiler of the Dead. When he has been killed, insure that he is not interred in a graveyard, if he is, be certain to place him face-down and place large rocks on his grave, or he will be quick up again and slaughter the graveyard's nighest neighbor.

the house in the woods

I don't know if the house in the meadows exists. I'm almost certain I've seen it outside of my dreams, but not sure enough to swear to it, never mind to actually wager. I could tell you that one summer evening, at twilight, I was walking on a dirt road lined on one side by a dense wooded area, on the other by an expansive field dotted with leaning, decrepit barns suffering from decades of disuse. The only sounds were my footsteps in the gravel, underscored by crickets' hypnotic chirping.

And I could tell you that I happened to look into the woods and saw the unmistakable shape of a Victorian, tall and narrow, surrounded and impaled by dense trees and thicket. I stopped short and let my eyes adjust to the gathering darkness.

I could tell you that the front door hung open, and that there may have been a source of light somewhere deep within the bowels of the place, enough to illuminate a carpeted front hall and steep staircase. I could say that the treetops were punched right through the roof of the place, that an ancient desk hung at a dangerous angle some yards above the house, perched upon an expansive asterisk of thick, knotted branches. That some clothing--a corset, a waistcoat, some giant white knickers--lay higher up, sagging from bowed branches as though hung there to dry.

And I could tell you I pushed through the underbrush and nettles and clouds of mosquitoes and then stood, scraped and bruised and bitten, in the front hall. I could tell you what shambled down the stairs, swinging an ancient watch on an ancient chain wound around ancient fingers. I could tell you what it said to me.

I could tell you so much, but I couldn't look at your face while I spoke.

I could tell you that when I returned to town, the streets were piled with caskets, centuries old and crumbling. That bleached, bloated arms reached from some. I could say that some of those caskets were tragically small. That some held the drowned, and leaked rank water that was waist deep and rat-strewn under the overpass.

That bodies impaled upside down on stakes filled the courtyard of my tenement, like an inverted audience waiting for a speech from a demented demagogue.

I could tell you of a rain of bruised babies slamming sickeningly into the pavement of the roads and sidewalks of Leeds, bouncing in dizzying numbers from the roof tops and canopies and awnings.

I could tell you that I was now a part of an army of the dead, whose instructions were dispersed by coded messages on a radio station. I could tell you of our foul mission and of our multitudes of intended victims.

I could tell you these things, my invisible audience, only on the airwaves of WXXT.

WXXT. If it bleeds, it's Leeds.

the arrival part 2

My name is Benjamin Stockton. It feels so good to say that. I am Benjamin Scratch Stockton. I have been effectively mute for over a year, scratching in dirt, penned in by a fence of wood and wire, eating hay for my filet and water for my wine. My diatribe was a wavering yell, my thoughts a stifled mass of black thunderclouds.

But yesterday, the day of the rains, was a big day, a mighty day. I was taken, brought into the wet woods under a slate-gray sky, and, brothers and sisters, I was born again. Born in blood in a dingy apartment on Eastern Avenue. But first I was given a message by a hapless messenger before I dashed out his brains in the grass with his own cane, now mine.

I have an apartment now, three rooms, sparsely furnished with leaning chairs, a solid table, a basic bed. In that apartment I ate meat again, and I turned on the television and, good people of Northampton, I watched my stories.

Then I lay myself down in the bed but could not sleep for the excitement. I put on the radio, a small transistor on a simple nightstand. I rolled the wheel to WXXT. They were playing the sounds of cats brawling, with cello. For six hours, I lolled happily in that hazy blur between awake and asleep.

This morning, I roam the town, seeing its changes, the ventures and enterprises that failed, the ones that are trying for the first time. Men and women walk the streets, the vulnerable and the damaged live there. They walk and they sit and they scream at passers-by but no one listens.

This morning, I watch a man drive a silver Impala from Pleasant Street, across Main, to King. He takes a left into the lot behind the Hotel Northampton. I cross at the crosswalk and enter the carpeted lobby. Sitting on a small, green-striped divan under a massive chandelier, I watch a ginger-haired, tall man lug two cases and a laptop bag to the front desk and check in. He glances my way and, momentarily disturbed for a reason I'm certain he cannot name, finishes the arrangements with the girl at the desk. A bellman takes his bags and stores them behind the counter, and he exits.

Now he walks, taking the measure of the morning, taking the temperature of the town.

I follow at an unobtrusive distance, taking the measure of the man, taking the temperature of the threat.

The man from the FCC has arrived. But so have I.

uncle red reads to-day's news

To-day on Petticoat Hill Road a half of a man split down the center edged from the woods weeping, reports Henrietta Swaggle. The man was baldheaded and emaciated, and left behind him a trail of teeth and innards. The most prudent and modest Henrietta says that the man asked in a most pitiful small voice for a cup of coffee before expiring in a state of inconsolable agitation and terror. A search of the woods turned up no additional remains.

Crestlawn Cemetery: the entire population of dozing denizens, numbering in the high tens, was apparently disinterred betwixt eventide and the Devil's Hour, rousted from their repose and removed, presumably, to parts unknown by an unidentified ghoul or ghouls. Gaping holes and yawing caskets remain, and the many footprints in the mud paint a most grim and unspeakable picture.

the leech

Among the most ghastly sounds a man can hear is the sound of a voice in what he thought was an empty house. That is what Todd Wessen heard on an early morning in his remote cottage on the edge of a tall wood. He woke before he knew what woke him, woke with a chill that ran from throat to bowel and back again.

Then he heard it again, heard it awake, a guttural sing-song, a wavering creak. Up he jumped, hitting every light as he passed from bedroom to sitting room, sitting room to hall, hall to parlor. Then at the doorway to the front room his foot stepped in wet. Before him in a patch of moonlight teetered a tall, silhouetted figure, bloated and awkwardly posed. It stepped into the light.

The man was purple, blue, black. His eyes were swollen shut; his nose a pimpled stone; his lips a blue ball bisected by a black blister of a tongue. A gray knot of bone jutted from his leg at the knee. He raised to the ceiling in an unfathomable gesture gnarled hands with fingers fused together with mold and rot. "We live deep down in the underwater towns," the figure burbled. "Our screams are bubbles, our fortunes drowned."

Then the abomination slowly opened a gummed eyelid.

Its red eye harbored a cloudy cataract that searched the room and found Todd's own eyes.

"I'm terribly sorry," the thing belched. "Can you point me toward the road to Prescott?"

Todd started to take a step backward, but something on the bottom of his foot prevented it reaching the floor. His foot flew out from under him, his left leg kicked up, and for a fleeting moment he was hanging in space. He landed on his back, hard.

Presently he regained his breath and propped himself up on his elbows. The empty room was bluish with dawn light, the floor dry.

A movement at his foot and he bent his knee to look. Clinging to his foot was a purple, bloated leech. It humped obscenely at the arch slowly, foully. It shrank and pulled, puffing up like the throat of a frog. He felt nothing at his foot, but he swore he could feel all the blood in his body pulsing towards his legs.

The next thrust pulled down his love, the next his memories, the last his mind.

He detached himself from the thin white man and inched along the floor, fat and round and deliriously full. The spines of his books loomed large above him like buildings in a cramped city, each letter too massive to read. He wept and he pulled himself forward and forward and then a shadow fell over him. He reared back his flat head and saw a pale foot descending. The thin, translucent membrane that was his skin burst and everything went red.

The thin, pale thing in the house gibbered and shook and trembled. It rose and opened the door and shambled down the walk.

the arrival part 1

*DAILY HAMPSHIRE GAZETTE - Four men with ties to
an occult group linked to human trafficking and ritual murder were
apprehended by State Police yesterday in the Hockanum Meadows and
charged with cruelty to animals and environmental crimes. The men
were in possession of packets of dried herbs and powders that have been
sent for testing, and of "The Libellus Vox Larva," a centuries-old
book all copies of which were thought to have been destroyed by the
1930s. Also discovered in the clearing were the mutilated bodies of
three of the four goats recently stolen from the Whipotte Farm. A fourth
goat could not be located. The men will be arraigned at the
Northampton courthouse on Friday.*

Along a line of reeds bent in a downpour, in the
meadows between the Connecticut River and the City of
Northampton, stands unsteadily on thick, slightly cow-
hocked hind legs a buck goat. Two horns jut from matted
white fur and curve to point back at his prominent shoulder
blades. A third, center horn spirals toward the sky in a thick
ribbon. He is loosely clad in dark trousers, a white shirt
soaked and translucent against the gray fur of his chest, a
dark vest and topcoat. A necklace bearing an inscrutable
emblem and ruby stone hangs at his chest. His eyes betray
bemusement, triumph, and a touch of animal irrationality

and volatility. His pointed beard is soaked into an inverted triangle, curled at the end. From the beard drips water and maybe a touch of blood, metallic and brown.

He takes a tentative step, now without trees to lean against for passage. Like a toddler finding his feet for the first time, he lurches headlong, his legs pushing into the earth as he propels himself along a raised path, then leaning back as he descends a grassy hillock down to the cul-de-sac that punctuates Eastern Avenue.

Down to even ground, as the rain lets up from a roar to a whisper, he walks more steadily, only a slight unevenness in his gait to give him away. He reaches the walk, and grins. Then he brays, a wavering tenor shout, his exposed teeth like a set of cracked wooden doors guarding a desecrated church.

He leans briefly on a silver Hyundai Accent, and then puts his upper lip to the antenna. His mouth opens as he takes in information. Then he moves East towards Williams Street.

A car speeds by in the rain, then brakes, shimmying, fish-tailing, coming to a rest with its front wheel up on the curb. One can imagine the driver adjusting his mirror. Then the car bumps down off the curb and speeds away south, tires squealing. The goat yells after it, eyes ablaze, cataracts reflecting the pulsing brake lights. He crosses Williams and continues past a long hedgerow, approaching a long, three-story row house with broad porches, each sharing two doors.

Onto the third porch from the second door limps a man, shabbily attired in a hooded sweatshirt and matted, worn corduroys, torn at the right knee, big white sneakers. The man is bearded, slender, with thick black eyebrows like caterpillars. He propels himself with a knotted, heavy walking stick with a gold handle approximating the body of a crouching panther with sharp teeth bared. The man laboriously descends the stoop, grimacing with each step.

He turns and faces the approaching goat, and he grins. "The agent arrives in the morning," he says. "At the Hotel Northampton."

The goat opens his mouth, his jaw nearly detaching, his mouth a gaping narrow cave. Inside is red and raw, the pink tongue, lined with fine tiny white hairs, vibrating as he cries out. The man's expression, previously one of perverse anticipation, falters. The goat raises one hoof, and the hoof bursts open in a pink cloud, sole and nail crumbling, raining down on the walk, revealing a pallid, prodigiously veined hand with gnarled nails encased in filth. The goat reaches out and grabs the walking stick by its handle, flipping it in the air and catching its tip.

He dashes it across the man's forehead, hard, shearing

down a large flap of bloody flesh, baring an expanse of skull-bone. A waterfall of blood pours down the man's face and front as he pinwheels his arms and crumples to the ground, spitting out bloody shrieks. The goat tilts his head inquisitively. "Help me," the goat cries out in a cracked and choked voice. "Don't leave me!"

Then he swings the walking stick sideways with a powerful arm, tearing open the man's cheek and sending teeth flying. The man looks up through all the redness but can't see the cane raised for the final blow. He feels his head come apart. His brains spray out on the grass. The goat pulls the body up by the hood of the sweatshirt and thumps him up the porch and into the dark apartment. The brains blacken with the rain. The blood washes into the grass. The neighborhood is silent again as the rain abates and dusk approaches.

Hours pass, from the apartment comes the sound of flesh tearing, muted screams. Finally, in the glow of the moon, a man stands naked, blood soaked, in the hall, piled at his feet are curved walls of furred flesh, horns and hooves, scattered ribs and broken legs and burst brisket. The slender man steps out of the carrion and enters a small bathroom. A toilet, a tub and shower, a towel hung over the doorknob. Moments later, he stands under the cascading water, blood and fur and bits of flesh swirling in a pink pool at his feet.

He steps out, pulls the towel around him. He regards his face in the mirror. His eyes are odd, each of his pupils a black, horizontal line. But he is young, or younger than he was when the FCC had sent their secret department's agents, who had discovered and destroyed WXXT's antenna; and their Sorcerer, who had taken away his voice and his humanity on a dark March night and banished him to a pen with idiot goats who stared and occasionally rammed his flanks with their hard heads.

"I am Ben Stockton," he tells the mirror.

uncle red reads to-day's news

Yesterday at twilight in Haydenville, the town Constable did report the sound of a childe singing a ribald song and saying macabre things deep in the sodden forest. Further exploration revealed a circle of mouldering mahogany and leather chairs entwined in the high treetops and a charred bassinet stuck half into an ancient Oak. Also located at the scene was a set of vegetable ivory buttons bearing inscrutable inscriptions and unholy designs.

the gathering in the deep wood

1

I was on a stool at the counter of the Look Diner, moving my scrambled eggs around the plate in the coagulating pool of ketchup and staring at my gray coffee, when the man walked in carrying his brain in his cupped hands.

The man wore a wrinkled gray suit over a pristine white Arrow shirt. He was of indeterminate age, with flattened dank hair and skin as white as his shirt. His mouth was agape, his eyes glazed with fear. He dropped down onto the stool next to mine, his legs slackening. Wordlessly, I slid over a bowl empty save a few tenacious flakes of dried oatmeal. Without acknowledging me, the man gingerly placed his brain in the bowl.

And so we sat as people around us ate and chattered and clinked their forks. Outside there was a violent stutter of thunder and the sky darkened as though somewhere a giant shade had suddenly been lowered.

I stole a glance at the man. The top of his head, just over the eyebrow, sat off kilter, like a hat just slightly askew. Blue stitches, inexpertly spaced, formed bridges over a thin wavering river of red bone. Tighter stitches toward the ear had squeezed out bubbles of brown blood, which had since hardened into beads.

A waitress rushing by stopped, and reached for the bowl. "Oh, I'm not quite finished," the man said in a polite purr, almost apologetically, and the waitress hurried on.

A cook with a broad brow reached up and spun the dial of the radio, which had been playing the greatest hits of the seventies, eighties, nineties and today, all the way to the left. The speakers thrummed with a low droning chord. The sky was blue-black. The clock read 8:05 a.m.

The man spun round on his stool to face me. Suddenly afraid, I stared straight ahead at the towering mountain of hashed potatoes. "ARE YOU LOOKING," the man intoned leeringly, "FOR A GOOD TIME?"

I have been asked that question, and variations thereof, as a boy, as a teenager, as a young man, and as a cipher of a man in middle age. I've been asked by a Cairo cab driver, a Panamanian pilot, a half dead priest in Prague, and a woman costumed as a koala bear on an impossible San Francisco incline. My answer has always been the same: No, but thank you.

But in the Look Diner, under a blackened sky, as people around us ate and chatted and clinked their forks, as potatoes piled toward the dingy ceiling, asked by a man who had come in carrying his brain in his cupped hands, as the radio droned with muttering, insinuating voices, as I could smell the spectre of death rising in plumes from my gray coffee, I said Yes, sir, if it will make you go away, if I don't have to look at your blazing eyes, if I could just be crouched under bedsheets a thousand miles from this cove of dark histories, I am...I am...looking...for...a...good...time.

He reached a long fingered hand into the inner pocket of his suit jacket and handed me a white flier folded in fourths. "Prepare for unspeakable pleasures," he cackled, and he plunged his face into the bowl. Slurping and snarling, he chewed and gnawed and gnashed, and his gray matter sprayed like ash, lighting on his browns, onto the counter. One sodden lump landed in my coffee and I slid from the stool and careened out of the diner, bellowing I know not what, the flier tubed up in my left hand, my right covering my eyes.

Trucks blared by on the road, their lights filtered red through my fingers. Then the rain came. Then the rain came. Then the rain came.

2

WXXT

in association with

Annelid Industries International

Presents

The Gathering in the Wood

The Slinkiest Nymphettes
Grotesqueries and Obscenities
Pizza and Pie

Featuring Original Music by the Notorious
EZEKIEL SHINEFACE QUARTET
and
DJ FESTERLY BOYLE

Follow the Lights

The Walk

At dusk I passed between the disused stone stanchions that once supported the gates to Mountain Park. A carpet of stony earth, an arch of orange leaves, an orchestra of peepers and highway groans.

There were streetlamps in the woods, among the trees, spaced as though lining both sides of a narrow road, though no road, no path, ran between them. Each was black iron, tall, topped by a light in an ornate glass cage clouded by mosquitoes and the occasional...bat?...no. The bodies were long and tapered, wormlike, and light shone through the black wings as though they'd been constructed of wire and crepe.

At length I felt and heard a beating bass line that made the forest floor vibrate.

I walked, pushing aside branches, kicking up bramble and prickerbush, waving away mosquitoes, clambering over dead-falls and felled trees. I thought of my wife, four months in the grave. For three of those months I had felt she walked beside me, guiding me, blushing at my tears and offering silent solace. That had been lost. Where had she gone? Now I wondered if she followed at my heel. Was she warning me away, or was it my own self, knowing no good could come of this venture?

Then, ahead, lights gleamed through the trees: pink and purple, red and orange, yellow and blue. I emerged into a clearing, in the center of which, angled oddly, sprawled a long, low building, the front of which was six broad garage doors with a horizontal line of frosted windows through which blurred colors pulsed in time with the punishing bass thrum. To my right, all the way past the last garage door, a narrow utility door stood propped open with a twisted, splintered crutch whose foot was buried in a cat litter bucket displaying a varietal garden of lipstick tinted cigarette butts.

I entered….

3

…into a cramped area with a carpet piled with shoes of

all varieties: oil-stained sneakers; bent high heels; flattened boat shoes; bedroom slippers; boots, some impossibly tall; slingbacks, clogs, and mules; sandals, birkenstocks, and flip-flops. To the pile I added my ancient bluchers. I opened a white, graffiti littered door and entered

Bay 1

In the center of the first bay were sprawled Chevrolets whose roofs had been sheared off. I looked up and saw that the roofs had been stapled to the upper walls and ceiling with huge, industrial sized bolts. Painted on the car roofs was artwork whose quality ranged from toilet stall stick figures with ungrammatical captions to stark, colorful, obscene Raphaelian frescoes to elaborate Carravagistian murals.

On one, a goat lay on his back in a lightning-veined thundercloud high above a vast, brown Mideastern city. The goat's navel was a dome light. Its jaw was slack, revealing long, wood-like teeth; its sinewy, muscled limbs were akimbo, its jutting sex about to be set upon by seven goggle-eyed cherubim with pink, pudgy, clutching hands.

At the corners, aged angels averted or covered their eyes, their expressions betraying distress or disgust. One had yellow streams of vomit shooting from her nostrils, her liver-spotted, heavily veined fingers entwined tightly over her mouth.

I made my way along the edge of the room toward a passage marked with bright blue duct tape. Through the doorway I thought I caught a furtive movement. My wife, leading me forward? The proprietor of the garage, delighted or repelled at its condition? The organizer of the heretofore missing "gathering" hinted at in the flier? I ducked through into

Bay 2

whose floor was piled high with discarded piles of clothing. Jeans dropped, forming a pair of empty eyes. Skirts and brassieres and crumpled tops, corsets, waistcoats, vests and undershirts. The walls here were lined with books whose spines spoke their titles in languages unknown to me. The few English titles appeared to be collections of aphorisms and/or instruction manuals by an Abrecan Geist. Moving toward the next doorway, opposite the last, I marked a few other upsetting titles in English.

Bastions of Disquiet, by Rangel Bantam
Violent Rigor, by Phillip Rippingcoat
Systems of Savagery, by Skelton Tornweather
Vistas of Carrion, by Carp Tarscallion
Aligning the Architectures of Deviltry, by Vasterian Cull

Suddenly a light finger touched my shoulder and I

whirled 'round. No one was there. I tucked in my chin and glanced rightward, and on my shoulder spied a house centipede the length of an unsharpened pencil on my shoulder. Its long legs danced as it scuttled toward my neck and I brushed it away with disgust. I looked up, and the ceiling was writhing with the foul creatures, a field of elongated, living burrs crawling on and over and around one another. I fled into

Bay 3

where finally I saw people--but these were children. None appeared to be over the age of five. Two boys were engaged in a solemn game of towering and then toppling blood-red blocks. A girl crawled over a large, flat book with blank pages, leaving blue ink hand and foot prints. An expansive crib rocked wildly, crowded with cooing babies. Strangely, the room was fairly quiet.

Across I saw a boy of about four in a striped shirt who looked vaguely familiar. He had wide-set eyes, light brown bangs drawing a fiercely straight line across his forehead, and small mouth set in concentration to match his furrowed brow. He was arranging on a green plastic podium an eight-limbed stuffed bear.

"What is his name," I asked.

"Tickles," the boy said. A line of pink drool swung

between his lower lip and the bear's round, gray ear.

"RUG-UH-HUM," a voice bellowed out over the diminutive crowd. "RUG-ugh-ugh-ugh-HEM," and I saw a boy of about 9--older by far than most in the room--hawk up a mass onto the white plastic table at which he sat, his knees up at his chin.

I set off in his direction, clamoring over children, toy dinosaurs, and navigating around a good sized pile of turds topped with a conical yellow party hat, rakishly tilted.

The boy looked up at me expectantly, eyes wide. The mass he had expectorated trembled on the table. It was pale gray and lined with what appeared to be pinkish veins. Though I addressed the boy, it seemed wise to keep a careful eye fixed on the thing on the table. This I did.

"Erm," I said, and then I stopped, unsure of precisely how to continue.

"Are you looking," the boy grinned toothlessly, "for a good time?"

I gaped at him.

"They are outside," he said. "The grown-ups. In the wood."

I looked back down at the table. The mass was gone. The lights seemed to brighten.

All the children, except for the sleeping ones, were looking at me, their eyes swimming with secrets.

I stood and headed for the exit.

uncle red reads to-day's news

Stolen from the Millside Church of the Most Holy Redeemer by the Hampshire and Hampden Canal: one (1) crucifix, two (2) pews, fourteen (14) hymnals (spines and covers only), three (3) jugs Holy Water, and the Private and Personal effects and papers of the venerable Father William Garrett Shineface; substantial reward for the return thereof, and for secrecy concerning the contents of the most holy and incorruptible Father Shineface's personal papers and diaries.

the sons of ben number 3

It always happened at the craggy precipice of sleep, so I never knew if it was a dream or a memory. I was swimming in brown water, terrified I might be swimming down...away from the surface. But then I would emerge, bellowing out breath, the water crumbling to dust around me, a flat steel sky with black-painted clouds above. I would crawl, then, through an askew city of rounded, flat, windowless buildings carved with unfathomable graffiti.

My elementary school, a few flat, one-story buildings connected by windowed corridors, lay across a narrow access road from the cemetery. A modest playground was situated by the inner curve of the road. I was making swirlies in the sandbox with my fingers when I first saw the tall man standing at the wrought iron fence. He was bald on top, long-haired, the hair a flat brown, damp. He wore tiny wire glasses that sat crookedly across a substantial and accusatory nose. A white shirt that showed shadowed ribs from under a dark grey waistcoat. He did not have to beckon with his long finger; his eyes, a brilliant blue, called me across the road. I was six. He could have been forty; he could have been fifty.

How did I know that he was my father? I had known

only that my mother was my mother and had been ѕѡ ҁ eternity. I had known forever that the man who lived with her could not have been my real father, though that was the charade. He treated me like a baffling stranger, and I was grateful for it.

He was vaguely unpleasant, and one sensed he was somehow...off. The armpits of his white striped shirts were perpetually stained. He spoke bumblingly, in a dopey and sing-song voice. He worked at and for the church in some capacity I never understood, and The Lord came first for him. Perhaps only for him. He seemed removed. His conversations with my mother were hushed and muted and few. They would read most nights; she her romances and he his worn Bible.

But the man at the cemetery was a vital man, a man who looked at the world with fire and at me with only embers, which I regarded as warmth. Warmth and excited recognition. The first time I saw him, as I said, I went to him across the road. He knelt and regarded me, grinning widely. I noted that behind his yellowed teeth was another full set of teeth--top and bottom, also yellow, also pointing this way and that. His gums were red and, below and above his canines, split to the bone.

He said to me that day the following: You must always take what you want, however you can. You'll find, he said, that once you are known for taking what you want, you won't have to anymore. It will be given to you freely.

Then he rose, not without effort, and strode away. I went back across the street and Mrs. Wisert looked at me quizzically and with trepidation. I shrugged and went in to fetch my coat and go home.

The next time I saw the man was not more than a week later. It was drizzling rain. He was by the fence again, and I rushed to his side. He told me I knew who he was. He said, I have some history for you. Listen carefully and do not speak. You were not born alone. You had a twin. I knew that one of you was good and one of you was evil. Like in a fairy tale. I buried the evil boy next to the mausoleum.

He gestured. The mausoleum was a small, windowless brick house with a pointed roof and a small crooked spire.

I only saw him once more, years later, as I was showing my new wife my old school. She was in using the bathroom, and I turned and there he was. He was grinning at me, but he turned and strode away when I approached. He looked like a giant bird to me, somehow, as though black wings would sprout from his back, and he would leap into the air, blotting out everything. He didn't. He merged with the fog.

I walked to where he had stood, and there was a transistor radio leaning up against the fence, rusted with age.

A window revealed squarish white numbers along a gray line, a red line bisecting the 8s most of the way to the left. I turned it on and his voice spoke through a squeal of static. "It's an an-teek," he said, drawing out and tasting the word.

When I was fifteen I went to the mausoleum and next to it found a patch of lighter colored grass. I had brought with me a shovel, and I dug as the crickets chirped all around me. The blade hit wood, and I pulled up a small box. I lifted the twisted, torn black clasp and raised the lid. The box was empty. But I remembered from long ago the inside of the box, the smell of varnish and the lines of light that glowed, glowed more faintly, and then disappeared.

uncle red reads to-day's news

Hatfield residents report the most unfortunate birth and early death of a baby girl whose features rested not upon her face but on her trunk. The yellowed eyes were set low over the lower rib, nose below the navel, and the most horrid, distended mouth at the juncture of the thighs. The girl was said to have made grave and horrifying prognostications and provocations in a bygone but yet discernible tongue before bearing the wrath of both mother and townsfolk. The Minister refused to bury the abomination in the Lord's cemetery, so the infant was interred in fire in the veriest remote marshlands.

Benjamin Throwbarrel of High Street reported a gaunt figure reclining in water drawn by his wife for her bathings. The intruder was fully clothed in greatcoat and a dark claret chesterfield, gaiters and doeskin gloves. Mr. Throwbarrel insisted that the man bore the bloated countenance, limbs and digits of the long-drowned, but that he reached from the clawfoot tub in a most suggestive and obscene manner.

Ye Gods, this rainy rotten morning brings nothing but horrid and ill-boding news. This day I will fetch my meals in a warm place, candle-

lit and full of my fellow townsfolk. I will avoid the woods and the narrow paths and shall steer clear of the gray, featureless men who leer from the park's dark edges. I advise you to do the same, dear, dear listeners.

You are listening to WXXT, the safe and secure home for your most impure thoughts. If we fail to mention the time and temperature at the top of every hour, no-one gives a diddling care, Mister Freddy Fungus-face.

the sons of ben number 2

I remember very clearly when my mother told me I was not adopted. The year was 1985. I was fifteen. I was standing in our yellow-green kitchen near the yellow refrigerator, staring at a painting of peaches and pears cradled in a wooden green bowl. "I am your mother," she said, plucking absently at her heroic perm. "Biological, and for real. Your father is not your father, but I am your mother."

I suppose I should have known that she was my real mother. We shared a resolute nose and wide-set eyes that, if they were any closer to our ears, would have rendered us unattractive, if not freakish.

What I don't know, even now, is the purpose of the deception in the first place. When confronted, she'd deflect the question or else proclaim that she "had her reasons." Presumably she had her reasons too for finally revealing the truth, and at that particular time in my (or her) life. I don't know if she thought through what the effect might have been. I hadn't quite reached the age where I was determined to find my real parents, and hadn't shown much interest. I was a quiet boy, liked trying to invent things, liked chasing animals around or proclaiming myself King of The Woods in a crown of construction paper, wielding a storm-tossed branch as some kind of vague weapon. But now I wanted to know about my real father. And there was no information forthcoming.

My mother, I knew, had played folk guitar. She was an idealist, and one of those quasi-hippies always hopping from cause to creed to church in lengthening cycles. I knew she'd sailed through minor cults and major communes, but had never become tethered to any. Perhaps she'd met the man in one of these places. I was determined to find out, somehow.

The night she told me, I dreamed vividly. I was lost, driving down a lonesome backwoods road in the dark of night, when through the trees I saw an orange glow. Cresting a hill, I saw that below me lay a massive city, not previously suggested by any signs or geography...just there, massive, in the leafy midst of the New England hinterlands.

In a blink, I was driving on a deserted highway amidst tall black buildings with windows glowing red and shadows dancing somewhere within. Alongside the elevated highway raged and roiled a black river, bisected by ornate, spired bridges that passed somewhere below the road on which I drove. Looming above the arches and the terraces, a large skyscraper seemed to rise before me, tattooed with an enormous, neon red inverted cross. Below the cross sprawled unreadable letters that looked vaguely Arabic.

The city was vast, lit red, save for blue lights that blinked in patternless intervals atop the taller spires and rooftops. Stone-winged cathedrals, with many stained-glass eyes, crouched like tarantulas amidst the skyscrapers. Cruel looking helicopters, noses angled low, roamed between the buildings like wasps. When I glimpsed the vapor-lit streets, I saw loose gangs of figures in strange configurations, several lone people scuttling like crabs into and out of crooked alleys. I saw shadows of things maddeningly large and unthinkably shaped where the corners of light met the shadows.

I became aware of the car radio, then. Classical music played backward, while a timpani raged and a voice muttered darkly in what must have been Old or Middle English. I remember being afraid to look at the passenger seat. Someone was sitting there, and it seemed vital that I not look, lest...lest what?

Would I lose control of the car and plunge into the oily river? Would I turn to salt or dissolve into corrosive sand? Would I go irretrievably mad? But I wanted to look. I thought that maybe my father sat shotgun, and that he knew where we were going. I looked, and there he was, tall, knees up, grinning at me through two layers of teeth under a voluminous mustache. He had short, neat hair parted severely on the side, betraying a thin line of grey scalp that curved like a scythe.

I saw that a leech was clasped onto his neck near the adam's apple, and it was pulsing. Jesus, Dad, I said, and reached over. I worked my fingers under the side of the foul thing, peeling it off of his cold skin, leaving a pattern of blue bruises. My father looked at me and gestured with his eyes. I put the leech onto my neck and felt it latch on, felt it beat like a fat black heart.

I blinked and he was gone, again, and he was back. He pointed, then flickered and faded away.

I followed the direction in which his bony finger had indicated, and ahead a bright light shone in the road, up where the lane split. I drove on, and between the north and southbound lanes a construction crew worked under daylight-bright industrial lamps. I saw them through a gauzy fog of dust and strong light...they wore blood-red vests and hardhats and massive goggles, and as the road sank I saw that the workers were bone thin, with skeletal jaws and long teeth. They labored on platforms over gaping holes in the earth, and among the men, piled atop rickety pallets, lolled babies, piles of them, in ashy cerements. I could not tell whether the crew was excavating or burying them.

The leech pulsed at my neck. I looked at my arms and they hung in flaps over my bones. I looked down and my legs were bones jutting under my jeans.

I snapped awake.

My mother stood above me. "Your father GAVE you those dreams," she said. "Learn from them."

I looked at her and closed my eyes again, fading against my will back into the dream. Now I drove in morning light on a curving road through verdant valleys and soft, lush hills. The passenger seat was mercifully untenanted. I heard a thundering sound in the distance, and as I crested the next hill I saw a herd of goats galloping madly over the grass, ridden by gaunt, decrepit angels with crushed and singed wings. The goats' eyes burned and seethed; the angels looked stunned, exhausted. Their faces were the faces of the demented and the doomed: shadowed, creased, despondent. Their eyes were black orbs that showed no whites, their slack lips thin and blue.

I tried to swerve, as did the herd, but try though I may I crushed two of their number under my wheels, and again I woke.

My mother was sitting beside my bed in her nightcoat, gnawing on her fingernails. Through her fingers she told me that my father's brother had died, and that we were to undertake what she termed a "purging" of the house.

the theories of uncle jeb

We used to sit with Uncle Jeb, Earl and I, and listen to him talk.

If you'd never seen a picture of a human skull, you could just gape at Jeb's visage--the skin was as though painted on, and a poor job done of it to boot. His frame was so narrow and slight that clothes seemed to weigh it down. Though he'd shiver like the dickens in winter, he never wore much beyond a pair of once-white overalls and a white tee with the sleeves torn off and the neck stretched out, as though at one point Jeb had had a trunk rather than a twig for a neck. His feet were twisted, repulsive abominations, purple and bulged, the toes elongated and bent to the right, the big toe all the way back against the swell of the forefoot, it's nail a pointed horn, like a goat's horn, textured and multicolored tapering into string almost all the way to the swollen red heel.

He'd tell us of his father, who would flatten frogs from the brook behind the house, and blow glass around their perfect-circle bodies, forming dinner plates. At first, he said, you could see the features of the frog, the division of arms and legs, the squashed eyes and tiny nostrils. Then it would deteriorate in its glass tomb, displaying the entire spectrum of colours. Then there would just be a pattern of gray dust. Once enough time had elapsed, he claimed, there would be nothing left. Just a glass plate. A LOCK'D ROOM MISTRY, he'd cackle. WHOLE STOLT THE FRAHGGY?

Jeb liked to tell us of his theories, and they were many and they were grim. He would hold up Gram's old Bible to the ulcerations on his pooched stomach, mark down the words that were bespeckled with blood, and tell us THAT was the real Bible, the hidden Bible, that God was Cancer and it spread through Man to help him but only destroyed him, and if Man only knew the Hidden Bible as he, Jeb, did, you could live forever with…and AS…cancer.

I AM Cancer, he'd intone, and he'd grasp the folds of his stomach, gaping wide his navel, which had never been properly tied off (according to Father), stretching it wide, a hole you could pop a child's head into (if you were of a mind), and the smell was low tide and sprawling arrays of fungus sprouting in the folds of a field of mildewed clothing, of dank basements and bile-strangled wells, carrion and the faeces of the squatting dead. I AM Cancer, he'd say again, AND I CANNOT BE BEAT. THE WORLD'LL BLACKEN AND SHRIVEL and be GONE.

That, Jeb said, would be the Kingdom of Heaven. Everything eaten by cancer, and the cancer eats itself, and then there's nothing and no one no more. Paradise, he'd whisper, his eyes squeezed shut.

When Jeb was in his cups, which thankfully was not often, he'd grab his overalls in a fist and yank them asunder. Then from his unders he'd pull out his I-can't-say-it, a confused grey mass of you-know-what, held together with a wet and reeking shoelace. THIS, he'd bellow, IS THE SOURCE OF ALL THE PROBLEMS IN THE WORLD. I USEDTA THINK IT WAS WOMAN BUT ITS THIS. He'd yank from his deep pocket a meat tenderizing mallet, heavy and dirty, and demand that we hammer his mess. I'd give a meaty whack or two, looking away in horror, to placate the lunatic. Earl, though, took to it. He'd wheeze his asthmatic wheeze and swing that hammer like a he-man at a carnival. Trying to ring the bell. BAMM, he'd yell. BAMM BAMM.

And Jeb would wince and groan and even cry, shuddering with every sick impact, but the whole time he'd be laughing, holding on with one wizened hand to a the rung of the chair behind him, the other hand digging ruts into the porch with its thick nails. Ah, he'd sing to the sky, ah, these'r good boys, and they'll take this town and make it their Kingdom. Then, sometimes, he'd vomit black tar that would roll down his chest like a waterfall and pool in his lap, and he'd pass out, and Earl and I would go down to the brook and kneel and say our prayers.

And the brook would be blood, and veined tumors would bob heavily in its roiling eddies.

uncle red reads to-day's news

Damnable days and dank dusks darken old Leeds in this foul Year of Our Lord Nineteen and Eleven. The cool nights provide little in the way of relief, what with muttering voices on the wind and ashy, two-heeled footprints on the hearth. My tea is an unnatural red color and my milk turns before it's a day cold out of the cow. It's enough to beat the Dutch.

Truth be told, I'm still a touch corned. And underslept. But I've been charged with telling you what's what and by devil, that's what I now shall do.

At the end of a thick trail of blood was found a Greenwich man with low-hanging dungarees and threadbare beard pushing a blood-sodden pram the contents of which cannot in good conscience be described. The man claimed the contents as his own son, somehow birthed without the womb of a mother. And bedamned if his torn and tattered shirt didn't reveal a belly dirked beyond exfluntication--hollow of organ or gland. His eyes, my friends and townsfolk, had no whites. And his tongue was a furrowed and chapped thing more dead than alive.

Old Margaret Melinda complained again of a stranger on her porch, proffering a bouquet of rusted distasteful trinkets. Narrow of chest and wide of belly, the man, she claimed, was clad in dank overalls and, worse, head-to-toe lousy with split and fruiting toadstool mushrooms. From behind his ears and under his arms they extruded, reported poor Margaret, and bulged from belly to groin to wide-set toes. Some were grained like wood and splitting; some bubbled with pinkish spittle and emitted malodorous and unspeakably foul spores that sickened the good woman and parched and wilted the flowers that hung from the eaves and filled the garden. The man was polite and well-spoken, and claimed to inhabit the cellars of the town.

A tortoise-shell cat in the Holyoke flats did kill Mr. Henry Floret, who before he expired exclaimed that the beast bore the eyes of man and spoke to him in prophecies of danger and ruin. Floret was bled dry and his corpse blew away in wisps and sheets on the heavy winds before the coroner could fetch it.

My tea is on the boil and it's been off the heat this whole time. The world is curdled and my shoes are all of the sudden too tight. I'm off to my nap. Don't come near me.

Don't come near me.

the last hike

God save us from girls who are into hiking, I used to say, until I met Janet. I resisted for a long time; I let her hike while I lounged on the couch; I gave her my old line about being an avid indoorsman...and she laughed it off, grabbed my hand, and dragged me in to the Massachusetts woods kicking, as they say, and screaming.

And who knew, but I loved it. It became our weekend activity, surrounding ourselves with trees, brooks, deadfalls, cliffs--all with a soundtrack of chirping birds and who-knows-what bumbling through the underbrush. I saw the morning sun bounce along the treetops and the evening sun make the leaves glow like orange-green fire. After a while I even became less convinced that our fate was to be eviscerated by bears. Not once did I even see a bear, though I did see a beautiful fox once, and another time, from a distance, a small mountain lion. I bought a backpack, boots, a poncho, a compass...hiking socks. Hiking socks!

Janet forbade our bringing phones, but she would bring a transistor radio, bless her heart. We would clear away twigs and brush and sit by the curve of a coruscating creek, eat peanut butter sandwiches, and listen to tinny classical music or operas from the UMASS station. It is only these memories of Janet--gone these many years--that I look back upon with anything like yearning. Not for her, sweet though she was, but for myself.

It was the radio, not a bear or a fall or a heart attack, that killed the man I was and stole the man I might have become. It is easier, somehow, for me to blame the radio. The surprising heft of the thing; the square, rusted speaker; the red vertical line all the way to the left of the green glowing dial; the dented, crooked antenna. It wasn't the radio, of course, it was Janet. She and the shadow that loomed just over her shoulder...tuning the radio to The Voice of the Mighty Connecticut. The Black Heart of the Pioneer Valley. 87.9. WXXT.

One week before we saw the man in the woods, we happened upon WXXT. We were enjoying a postprandial laze, listening to Handel's *Tamerlano*, when a wave of static washed over the music. Janet fiddled with the dial, easing it leftward until the aria resumed...only to be again obscured by white noise. A millimeter to the left once more and a voice spoke, clear and loud, as though the announcer were standing between us. I literally threw my iced tea into the air.

MUSIC FOR THE SICK, bellowed the voice, resonant, compressed, with a slight echo. GATHER TO YOUR

RADIOS! COME TO MY VOICE, ILL AND UNKEMPT, RIDDLED WITH CANCERS, CRAWLING WITH PESTILENCE! TOUCH THE SPEAKERS WITH YOUR HANDS! AH! THERE! YES! Then the voice sank to a conspiratorial tone, almost a whisper. Janet inched up the volume. *All of you weary and morose, despondent and despised, pickled and petrified, abused and abandoned! You are listening to Willard Vincent Winklepleck of the Warwick Winkleplecks! Your healer and your servant, your shaman and your hero, your familiar...and your friend. My pulpit is your preserve, my altar your asylum, my chancel your comfort! Come to me! Step over the trancep...* I shut it off.

And Janet turned to me with seething hatred in her eyes, a thing I had never seen in a year of knowing her and did not care to see again. "Religious crap, " I said, with a whining, defensive tone in my voice that I was instantly embarrassed by. "What are we, in the deep South?"

Listen, said Janet, with the whispered reverence of the zealot, and she turned the radio back on. It was music now, that fearsome voice gone--but WHAT music! Violin bows shrieked against untuned strings in a furious frenzy. Bass notes climbed and descended drunkenly, causing a dizzying, disorienting sensation that reminded me of an inner ear infection. Guitars were in play too, fighting off abusive, obtrusive hands and other...parts...and beneath it all a rising, implacable, impending drone that seemed to fill the woods, darken the sky, still the thrushes, curdle the cream in our cooler. I fainted dead away...

...and awoke with Janet above me, her face creased with concern. The only sound was birds. She touched her hand tenderly to the back of my head and drew it back with blood in the whorls of her fingertip, then she felt around and said she couldn't find a wound. I felt strange, off-kilter, but physically unhurt. Not saying much, we hiked home in the reddening dusk.

* * *

The next weekend we set out again, driving through Southampton and Westhampton and into the woods somewhere beyond Huntington. We parked on the curve of a deeply shaded wood, grabbed our gear, and started walking through an expansive field. At the field's end was a wall of impossibly tall pines, like a wall concealing a secret city. The treetops were a child's frenetically penciled scribble across an expansive painting of a bruise. The tree trunks were sprawled, glistening, mottled with black lichen in intricate patterns, looking for all the world like malignantly eschatological graffiti. The ground around them was thick with varicose roots twining through, around, and over soft mushrooms the size of chair cushions. Some of them were partially collapsed or split with gaping fault lines, revealing their inner craggy textures. They seemed to breathe out a pulsing fog, fetid, fusty. I pulled my shirt up over my nose. We climbed over the roots. At one point my boot slipped through and plunged into one of the mushrooms and I had to fight off nausea. We disappeared into the woods and whatever daylight had been evident disappeared along with us.

* * *

In the intervening week I had become a devoted listener to WXXT. I did not tell Janet. I don't know why. She had seemed so intent on making me listen that day in the woods, but had not brought it up since I passed out. I'd leave for work, call in sick from the car, park on the shoulder of 202, and listen all day. I heard Captain Calumny's Rockabilly Riot; twisted, imperious, impious sermons by a crusty-voiced preacher named Ezekiel Shineface; prolonged psycho-sexual confessions by announcers with names like Benjamin Stockton, Guy Stanton, Rivven Stallhearse, and Rexroth Slaughton. One day I listened for four straight hours to a four word mantra repeated over and over again (I forget what it was). On another day I listened to an hour of someone very realistically pleading for his life, set to jaunty polka music. Occasionally there were percussive bleats that made it sound as though the victim was being violently assaulted with an accordion. I heard dirges and Satanic hip-hop, monologues and weeping. I heard strange and upsetting news items read by an Uncle Red. Thursday, a day of crashing thunder and strong winds, I heard only whispers. I could not make out the words. I listened all day.

I'd arrive home at my usual hour, as though I'd been to work. We'd plod through our evening rituals: take-out, television, video games on the Wii. I was withdrawn and distant. My head was swimming with the day's broadcasts. Janet was patient, affectionate, almost doting. I thought it was she who suspected nothing.

* * *

We hiked through the late morning through deep deep woods, up and down steep inclines choked with dead branches from the October snowstorm. We inched along a dizzying cliff edge with coiled chains and disused, leaning stanchions the only protection from a surely fatal fall. The roaring river below was muted to a whisper. At one point a cat fell into step with us. He was black with a white throat. He looked up at me companionably then, after twenty minutes or so, split off into the underbrush. Janet began to rhapsodize about nature's violent beauty and I listened raptly--it sounded like a monologue one might hear on

WXXT. We ate in a clearing. I was ravenous. My sandwich and crackers gone, I wet my fingers and pulled up crumbs from the cooler. "Try these, they're OK," Janet said, plucking a few violet, bulbous berries from a string of black vines. The vines wound abundantly around the base of a fat-trunked conifer, appearing to squeeze the tree into an almost feminine shape. I ate the berries and they burst soft and bitter in my throat. They tasted finer than the finest wine I'd ever drunk.

I stood to survey the area--and I saw the man at the far edge of the clearing. He was standing on a flat rock, like a boatman on a raft on a still river. He was tall, very tall, thin. The wind kicked up the dead leaves around him but his herringbone ulster hung lifeless. From a distance his eyes were black circles without pupil or sclera. His mouth was hidden in a slack grey beard. He raised his long arms and I heard that familiar rising drone. Janet had put on the radio.

The man's fingers were long and many-jointed. They bent this way and that, forming staircases and many sided shapes and lightning bolts. They danced, and the leaves danced. The wind ululated in time and the clouds thickened and metastasized and wheeled, wheeled, wheeled like eddies in brackish water.

I am Willard Vincent Winklepleck of the Warwick Winkleplecks.

More men emerged from the trees, grey men in grey coats with grey faces.

I am Janet Combs-Tonkin of the Prescott Tonkins.

The man shed his clothing and the other men followed and they were cobwebbed and cadaverous and carrion-curdled.

I am Benjamin Scratch Stockton of the Swift River Stocktons.

The cat from the path meandered among the men, rubbing his tooth on their grey knees, and the men began to chant.

I am Jebediah Blackstye of the Enfield Blackstyes.

We walked towards the men, across the windswept clearing, shedding our clothes.

Of course, we weren't called WXXT in those days.

As we approached, we saw that the grass was wet with blood.

We were a ragtag band of miscreants, dopers, murderers, witches, bitches, baristas, smugglers, thieves, bandits, veterinarians, panty-sniffers, harlots, Jews, pederasts, dim-wits, and sneaky-Petes.

It ran in rivulets between our toes.

Obliquely worded news-paper advertisements led us into the woods on that September day, written by no-one knows who but designed to draw precisely the crowd it drew.

I spoke words in a language I did not know.

Over 100 years later, well beyond our bodies' meager lives, we broadcast the Word from the woods of Leeds.

I slipped in blood and fell onto a discarded topcoat that wriggled and hissed, alive with fat pink worms.

I am Guy Stanton of the Shutesbury Stantons.

Then six black vans motored out of the woods, their engines roaring over the deafening drone of the radio. The windows were tinted. Three of the men hoisted me from the ground. They lifted me over their heads, these deranged, dead-eyed pallbearers, and propelled me toward the nearest van. I tilted my head back, upside-down, and saw Janet. She was standing on the flat rock, the grey man behind her, his hands on her shoulders. They were both grinning, their eyes aflame. The family resemblance was unmistakable.

Then I was in the van's pitch interior. It smelled of pungent sweat. I sat in one of the seats. It was damp against my bare skin...not damp, waterlogged. A young man was seated beside me, stunned and wall-eyed, more young men behind me in the darkness. The driver, clad only in huge mirrored sunglasses, turned and grinned a toothless grin. I saw my face and other faces, angled and elongated in the reflection. He said, "Anyone mind if I put on the radio?"

You are listening to WXXT, Wormtown's Winningest Wadio Station. Join us after the break for the Silvery Sounds of Silverfish Slinkard and his Slippery Symphony.

pharaoh

The boy stood at the edge of the playground, his thumb worrying the corner of his mouth, the fingers of his other hand squeezed into the diamond-shaped hole of the chain link fence, his red hair tousled by the wind. Like that he stood for some time and then quite suddenly and for no discernible reason turned and ran, kicking up dirt clouds, like the devil was chasing him. He nearly collided with Mrs. Haggerty, who was standing by the swing-set in a stance expressly designed to stave off disorder. Aside her, three girls swung up high, swooped down, and up again, laughing, their little feet kicking at the clouds.

"The pharaoh has a dust on his head," the boy announced.

Mrs. Haggerty bent and put her hand on top of the boy's head and rearranged his hair. "Stanley," she said. "Do you know what a pharaoh IS?"

Stanley knew this one. "A bird!" he squawked, in that childish way that sounded like "a bowed."

"Is the bird hurt, Stanley?" she said, emphasizing the "r" sounds in the third, and then for good measure the fourth, word.

One shrieking boy chased another between them and

she grabbed the chaser by his sweatshirt hood. "That kind of laughter swiftly turns to tears," she said in practiced sing-song, letting him go, then, again, to Stanley, "Is the bird hurt?"

"No, he's over there!"

Stanley turned and pointed, and Mrs. Haggerty stood and put a horizontal hand to her brow to block the afternoon sunlight. Beyond the chain link fence, at the edge of the woods, a man in a bird mask stood. He was wearing a matted overcoat and large boots, his hands concealed in long grey gloves. She adjusted her hand slightly and gasped. The mask was startlingly realistic. Layered brown and black feathers, a wide yellow-white beak that ended in a sloped point, piercing round green eyes. The man's head twitched in the mask, looking all about, like a few frames had been edited out of the film. As the boy had indicated, a long tendril of dust lay across the top of the head, down over one eye, its end floating dreamily in the air.

As she watched, the man turned and strode into the woods, struggling not at all with the tangled underbrush. Mrs. Haggerty felt a chill. Stanley tugged at her sleeve. "The pharaoh said it's all ending," he said.

"Wh..." Mrs. Haggerty started. Not at what Stanley had said, but at the silence. The playground was empty. She looked and the children were all walking into the woods, their colorful clothes fading as they entered the darkness. Red dust fell from the treetops and the birds in the woods began to screech as though panicked.

A cloud smothered the sun and the shadow slid over the swing-set, the see-saw, the spring riders, the slides and climbers, until all was shaded and dark. The trees shook.

Mrs. Haggerty turned to run to the school and the bird man was there, behind her, right behind her. He raised his arms and opened his beak and the sound was that of the end of the world and her voice rose to meet its timbre and it was a shrieking duet of death.

You're listening to WXXT. Now, the Swift River Sallies with their stirring rendition of "Shall We Gather at the River."

great uncle eltweed

When the call comes, it's never at a convenient time. In this instance, it was at 4 p.m. on a rainswept Saturday in late November. My great uncle, having lived to the improbable age of 102, had apparently finally worn down the staff at Brookside Willow Pavilions with his increasingly loud and incoherent and doleful jeremiads, and the Board of Directors had voted to unceremoniously "release" him. I argued on the phone, employing every cliché (where is he supposed to go, you can't do this, etc.) and inventing some new ones.

But I understood from the start the effect on people my uncle could have, even when well. After all, as long as I'd known him, his ideologies and religious affiliations changed like the New England weather, and each change came with an oft-repeated speech. The man couldn't go a month without a new epiphany. And rather than gather the family 'round, he'd corner you at a reunion and regale you with the speech you'd heard him give Aunt Asenath at breakfast. Verbatim almost, but with each new iteration a change here and there...a comedian "improving" his act. He'd even execute a self-deprecating laugh or a knowing shake of the head...at the same spot each time.

The person on the other end of the phone was a dispassionate, obdurate bureaucrat with a resonant voice-- an old time broadcaster's vibrato. No, the decision had been made and was final and I, as the sole heir to this particular misfortune, had no choice but to drive from New York up through to central Vermont to fetch my great uncle and his meager belongings. Now. And he had no one left but me.

A few phone calls to work and family across the ocean, and I was off. I drove between the sodden trees and frowning awnings lining East 79th Street and wended my way through the drizzle-hazed, Creamsicle-coned streets, and onto the FDR. By the time I hit 95 North, the drizzle had stopped but all was still black and white. The radio-- alternating between talk and music--kept me company and awake during the first part of the trip up through Connecticut, then I added a strong, large coffee somewhere south of Hartford. A duo, I thought, coffee and radio, working to keep my car on the road.

But then, a few miles before the border of Vermont, the radio bailed on me. A rental car without satellite or a CD player is what you get when you call at 4:30 p.m. on a weeknight, and that's when I'd called. So now, as night really settled in, and the coffee began to wear off, I settled into a serious fret. I needed more coffee, but I couldn't remember the last time I'd seen an exit, or a highway sign for that matter. But I resolved to keep going, and I did, pretty much until the point when I realized that going back to the last exit with Food signs would put me too far off schedule...and I wouldn't be able to do it anyway until another exit came along. So, if no coffee...I spun the radio dial back and forth melodramatically, finding only varying keys of buzzy static. I cranked the volume, hoping the static might form into music or words.

I didn't care what I would find--talk, sports, any kind of music. Just a voice, please, or a musical note. A zither's strum, an accordion's bleat, the plastic thump of an electronic drum...a goddamned SOUND. For five minutes straight I begged the radio aloud, just to hear my own voice...and then the dissonant chord of a church organ sounded so clearly and loudly that I briefly lost control of the car. Someone watching would have thought I'd had a stroke, I thought, but the idea of someone watching in the middle of nowhere, from the towering woods...well, that was something I didn't want to think about. I wrested the car back into the travel lane with one hand and spun back down the volume with the other.

"Through him...in him...with him...in the unity of the holyyyy spiiiiiriiiii..." warbled a male tenor, a very familiar doxology, though I hadn't been in a Catholic church since the age of thirteen. Then the priest's voice faltered, rasped, and disintegrated into a violent coughing fit...wet, hacking, productive coughs, by the sound of it. On and on it went, until the reel-to-reel at the station must have begun to fail. The cough slowed to a low, monotonous drone, then sped up slightly, faster, chirpily fast...then reversed...backward coughing for a time, then backward singing, with that lispy, hissing sound like the tongue of a serpent caressing the microphone with unspeakably foul intent. Then the loop stopped as though the reel had been violently dispatched, and after some thumping and clacking, organ music resumed, a climbing, sing-songy, carnival tune. Occasionally it reversed for a time and then righted itself, providing a disquieting soundtrack as I drove through the dark night, the walls of the woods rising higher and higher on either side of the unlit interstate. I still hadn't seen any highway signs. Even the painted stripes were gone. Blacktop, woods, moon.

The road does tend to hypnotize one, and it certainly did me. I fear I slept awake, dreaming and driving, for exactly how long I'm afraid to speculate. What woke me up, I thought, was drums...which is an odd accompaniment for pipe-organ music, to be sure.

But then I looked to my right and saw two reined and harnessed black horses galloping madly alongside, kicking up gravel. The hooves were bass drums, the gravel tapping my window was tom-toms and snares. The nearest horse's eye rolled toward me...it was red-veined and wide, and full of terror. I hit the accelerator. Their muscled torsos strained in the moonlight as they began to pass me, their heaving sides, their lashing tails...and then a black stagecoach, shaped like a squared-off heart--a curtained window; a low, windowed door; another curtained window. On the roof, strapped-in luggage, ancient and tattered. My car swelled with sounds: pipe organ, rising, rising; the thundering hooves and ricocheting gravel, the creaking, clattering carriage; the hysterical whinnying.

Then ahead, I saw a street sign, the first I'd seen in miles. It was a red, reflective diamond and it read, BUMP. My car, and then the carriage, hit what felt like a ramp. My car left the ground and slammed back down. I heard a tire go. Alongside, the carriage rose and descended. When it came down and hit the pavement, the door flew off, hitting the rear of my car and spinning into the darkness. Spokes cracked and flew from the tires, splintering as they hit the pavement. One speared a horse in the flank, and it shrieked horribly as blood spurted in a great arc. The trees blurred by, smudged thumbprints smeared over impenetrable thicket.

Then the whole carriage leaned like a house of cards, squealing, nails popping, faults gaping between the boards.

I saw with mounting horror what had been revealed when the curtains were torn from the windows. In the front, in the driver's seat, was a goat with nubs for horns and giant, gravestone teeth. I'm going mad, I thought. The goat wore a tall hat. A monocle on a chain sat over one eye. As he struggled, his hooves pummeling the wheel, I saw beside him another goat, shrieking, one ear soaked in blood, massive teeth, wide eyes. Lipstick was smeared ineptly about its lips. It wore a woman's frock and pearls. Then the horses began to gallop faster, and I saw into the rear window. Man and woman, human, middle-aged, freshly dead, their hair and jaws bouncing in time to the careening carriage, their purple tongues swollen, protruding from their mouths. Their teeth were shattered, their eyes staring, unseeing. As I watched, the carriage disintegrated, goats and humans spilling into the road like dolls in the wreckage. The couple was naked from the waist down. Suitcases skittered across the road, opening, spilling clothing. The wounded horse pushed out its front legs straight, and they broke with horrible cracking sounds. The horse collapsed, and the other dragged his partner hitchingly into the darkness, their shrieks echoing through the trees.

I stopped my car and sat in silence. The radio was quiet, my heart beating madly, pushing at my ribs. I opened the door and stepped out onto the highway. It was suddenly so quiet and still...just the sound of one detached wheel rolling in decreasing circles at the shoulder of the road. And then I saw the faces...in and among the trees...children, mostly, some young adults. Their faces were white...a grim diaspora of the damned. The wind ruffled the leaves and their hair. They were whispering, all of them. It sounded like rain. I walked toward them, and they faded back into the woods as though the group all had slid quietly backward into the dark. I continued until I saw them again...and they faded again. And again. And again. I trod through the underbrush, my shoes squishing in the mud, until after about ten minutes I saw a dull yellow glow. I followed the glow into a small clearing. Ringing the opposite side, the faces hung in and among the trees, gape-mouthed.

Before me hovered three goats bathed in moon-glow, the middle one slightly higher than the others. They wore dulled red and white robes, and their expressions were beatific. Flies buzzed around them, lighting and then taking off, lighting again. The middle goat's forearm was pointed at the sky, her hand the delicate, small hand of a young woman. Her middle and forefinger pointed up, the ring finger and pinky pointed down, against her soft palm. Her feet dangled from the bottom of the robe, toes wiggling absently. Her goat's mouth quavered, and then the jaw moved up and down as though she were speaking. I lent forward, but heard nothing except the filthy buzz of the horseflies. Her eyes, those queerly shaped goat pupils, fixed upon mine and held them. Then she grinned, all huge teeth and blister-flecked tongue. Her eyes blinked heavily.

They rose, the three of them, up into the fog, and were gone. The grey faces faded back into the trees. Whatever this was, it was over, no word spoken. I returned to the car. It started, and I drove away, slowly, the radio off.

Before long, I saw lights lining the highway ahead, and soon an exit sign. I walked into a Sunoco's too-bright food mart. On the radio a woman over-emoted to generic R&B. I went into the restroom and regarded myself in the mirror. My hair stuck up in spikes, and the familial dark circles around my eyes were darker than normal. Otherwise, I was me. For whatever that was worth. I splashed my face with water, grabbed a limp sandwich smothered like a murder victim in plastic wrap, and got back on the highway.

An hour later I exited the highway in Central Vermont, the mountains looming high above me. I drove through a sleeping suburban complex of wide, white houses with broad porches, some surrounded by expansive and neat hedges, and turned into the driveway of Brookside Willow Pavilions. I got out of the car. My legs were shaky and I felt very tired and overwhelmed. It felt like a chore just to walk.

I opened the double doors.

The lobby was empty. A desk with a phone and a computer was angled in the middle of the room; to the left of that on a podium sat a guest register with a few scribbled names and times. There was no receptionist in sight. Somewhere down a hall echoed upsetting percussive sounds I could not identify. I signed my name and that of my uncle--Eltweed--and started down the hall toward the crashing sounds. The door to Section C, where my uncle resided in one of fifteen cheerless bedrooms arrayed around a grand piano and constellation of chairs, had a light brown handprint on it. I somehow immediately identified it as butterscotch pudding. I opened the door, and the crashing sounds stopped.

The lounge area, usually buzzing with residents reading the paper or nodding in front of half-done jigsaw puzzles or staring into space, was empty. I saw no aides or servers. Magazines lay fanned out on end tables. A dying flower sagged in an empty, dusty vase. Then I heard a titter from the dining area. I went around the piano and into the L-shaped room.

My uncle sprawled in a large easy chair where the dining room table was supposed to be, clearly quite dead--a mannequin conceived in a madhouse. What was left of his grey hair formed a cloud around the back of his head. His jaw hung at his chest and his eyes showed only whites. He was clad in a fly-blown bathrobe and striped boxers whose front lay alarmingly open. Between his feet sat a transistor radio, spitting staticky gypsy jazz. Sitting on each of his wiry, bare legs was a dark-skinned aide. One was plump, in tight fitting grey sweats. The other, in an evening dress, was wasp-waisted and hard-faced. Both were Dominican, both grinning wickedly. The plump one looped her tongue over and around his large left ear, and then bit, hard. My uncle came to life, his eyes rolling back into place, and cackled. He stood, and the nurses clambered off of him and, holding hands, retreated, swiveling exaggeratedly through the double doors that led to the kitchen. "My boy," he said, softly. Then he clapped his hands.

"Get this," he said, and he cleared his throat. The voice that came from him then was not that of my uncle, but was instantly familiar in its exaggerated officiousness: "I'm afraid your uncle's time at Brookside has come to an end."

It was the voice from the phone.

"Uncle L," I said. "What's..." I couldn't quite find the words. I think you'll forgive me.

"Did they come to you?" he asked. His tone was one of whispered reverence. On the highway?

"They did," I replied.

Did she speak to you?, he asked, and it came rushing

back. The words spoken by the goat, in the clearing in the woods by the dark highway, in the glow of the moon. I heard them now. I smiled.

Come with me to the chapel to pray, he said, and reached out a hand red and blue, all the skin shrunk to the bone as though pulled taut and bruised in the process. His hand was, as it always had been, powerful, strong. It was like grasping some ancient scarab. He led me down a reddening hall.

The chapel was small and lined with faded tapestries. It consisted of ten wooden pews facing an altar backed by a giant crucifix, shaped in such a way as to suggest it loomed over the room, the top wider than the bottom, fanning towards the corners of the ceiling. Atop the altar, something squirmed and pulsed under a white cloth. We knelt before the pew in the back. The room was illuminated only by scant track-lighting on the high ceiling and red tealights that lined the arms of the crucifix. I could see hulking shapes silhouetted in the pews, but could not identify them. My uncle spoke.

The sun has fled to warm more worthy places, he said. Quartus! Medad! Lemuel! (The names of his brothers, grown, dead, buried, gone to dust, all long before my birth. I had seen them only as wiry, sinister blurred men in cracked, black-clouded tintypes.)

The shapes in the pews began to quaver. I heard the

buzzing of flies, the splitting and tearing of flesh.

Through him, with him, in him...

The room, which had smelled vaguely of cedar, now filled with a mephitic stench: carrion, cancers, bubbling rot, exploding tumors, sour decay. Stinkhorn, collybia. Foul motes swarmed like ticks above the tea lights. The room went all green and I retched piteously.

I am quite mad, my uncle allowed. We must leave this place. There is an army to command, soldier, and I am for the earth. He paused, and then his eyelids lowered and his eyes rolled back. He grinned, his tongue flicking the corner of his dry mouth. What did she give you?

"Who, uncle?" But before I'd finished the question, I felt the weight in my coat pocket. I'd felt it since I'd got back in the car. I reached in and pulled out the knife. It curved and glistened, serrated to pull at innards when withdrawn--to mutilate, to devastate. In the green light, I felt my eyes sliced open and drained, and new eyes grew like mushrooms in their place. Somewhere back in the residential quarters, that mad percussive sound began anew. I turned and mighty horses stood before me, their eyes wild. One, paler, leaning, stomped irritably and shrieked.

To Leeds, my uncle cried, and the building unfolded like

110

a flower.

the investigator

The man in the sopping overcoat fumed beneath an awning that drooped under punishing, pounding rain. Even given the immediate circumstances, he looked pointedly desolate, perhaps despairing, most certainly far from home. And far from home he was. A freelance investigator contracted by various government agencies, he had been sent by representatives from the Federal Bureau of Investigation and the Federal Communications Commission from the hum of D.C. to this remote New England town for a very strange assignment indeed. Strange and unprecedented. His having been caught in this downpour, blocks from his rented car, felt like what his father, now five years in the grave, would have called the bitter end. Charming little town, though, yes, certainly, sure. For three weeks and counting he'd eaten charming meals in charming cafes, browsed in charming boutiques, strolled a charming college campus, looked out charming windows at charming people. He, Clem, for that was his name, was decidedly all charmed out.

For one, he could not locate on the dial the rogue radio station he'd been sent to investigate. Not at 87.9, not at 88.3, nowhere down that lonesome, echoing end of the dial.

And adjust that dial he did, by hair-widths and fractions, over a period of weeks, hearing only lead-voiced news anchors, tinny polka, or just static. No ghostly voices, no whispered exhortations to murder the hotel staff, neither murmured incantation nor perversion of prayer. Once he thought he'd found it, when he'd hit upon a humming drone that had rattled the speaker of his transistor radio. But then the hokey tone of a banjo plinked, plonked, plinked and a hammy Henry and a simpering Liza began bickering exuberantly about the manner in which they might solve the problem of a defective bucket. The voices, which bubbled and burbled as though the singers were gargling, seemed somehow to foul the room. He'd switched off the transistor in annoyance...and fear? Why would he feel a touch of fear? He'd tried that station again periodically, something itching at the back of his brain, but it seemed to have the cloying little tune on a loop. That must pull in the advertisers, Clem thought. If they'd just announce the call letters or the frequency, he could report it, could actually have something to show his client, to indicate he was actually earning his keep. There's a hole in the bucket. Dear Liza. Dear Liza. A hole.

One thing he *had* detected, in his monitoring of the local newspapers and the free weekly, was a very small but growing unease. A lurid feature in the weekly exacerbated that unease, with its tales of disappearing sons and daughters, supposedly lured away by charismatic voices on the radio, voices that spoke reassuringly to outcast teens, promising spiritual succor illicitly entwined with libertine allures. Absent a sample recording, Clem had nothing on which to proceed save the accounts in the paper. These accounts, if genuine, were proffered anonymously, and the reporters were predictably obstinate about protecting their sources. Silliness, thought Clem. "Sources." These small time reporters dreamed daily of proudly blockading a government entity, and he was providing them, by proxy, the realization of that fantasy. He worried that this city might soon have a hysteria on its hands. He had followed with some interest the recent news stories of a small town in New York state, many of whose teens simultaneously began suffering convulsions and uncontrollable verbal outbursts.

In the slim dossier given him by his contact, an Agent Schwaller, were accounts of the disincorporation and subsequent flooding of several towns to make way for the Quabbin reservoir, and of the Mill River flood whose wrath all but destroyed several towns in the area. There was also a brief history of occult activity in the area dating back to the founding of the town in the mid 1600s, though the connection with the immediate case was never stated. The cases dealt largely with disappearances, ghastly incidents of cemetery vandalism, and frightful wraiths accosting travelers walking unaccompanied on lonely paths. As the years passed, the incidents were fewer, or at least less frequently remarked upon, until they all but ceased in the mid-1970s. Later in the town's history the local Insane Asylum had housed several townsfolk affected by these encounters. But the Asylum had been closed during Reagan's reign, its inhabitants dispatched unceremoniously into the streets. The last of the untenanted brick buildings had been cleared to make way for featureless condominiums, and their former denizens were either dead or doddering. So Clem's focus was on the rumors of transmitters in the woods of nearby Holyoke, Williamsburg, and Leeds. Apparently the wraiths had found the encroaching populations and the attendant construction made for fewer lonesome paths, and had turned to the airwaves. Well, why not?

It seemed damned futile, though, searching the endless, storm-tossed woods for a transmitter, walking around with this hulking piece of equipment that looked like some manner of ancient Geiger counter. The woods are beautiful but beauty, like charm, sustains one only so long. To date there was no transmitter found and two pairs of shoes ruined, and by God he would expect reimbursement from the Federal Communications Commission. Reimbursement with interest...and a written apology. As he smirked at the idea, a cold drop of water hit the back of his neck. In a sudden fury he danced a ridiculous angry jig, his Brogans slapping the pavement, and at the height of his performance his glasses flew from his face, skittering across the sidewalk. The rain applauded enthusiastically. Too annoyed to feel shamed, he bent with a grunt to pick them up, wiped the lenses on his tie and placed them gingerly atop his nose...

...and on doing so he looked across the street at a two-story, brick commercial block. Outside a glass door was a small array of books on a folding table getting soaked, ruined. The sign above the door said ANNE GARE BOOKS. Feeling as though a measure of altruism might salvage something in this day, maybe in the whole trip, he scudded, hunched, across the road, hoisted the table, and used it to push open the flyer-choked glass door of the book store. A bell dinged as he pushed through. He slammed down the table, heavy from the weight of the sodden books. Over the din of the rain, now muffled somewhat by the closed door, he heard laconic pipe organ music from the speakers at the corners of the shop. Behind a counter ringed and towering with books and papers, he could just about see the back of a man's head leaning heavily forward, as though he was dealing with something or another on the floor or on a low shelf. The man's hair was long and tangled and wet. He was probably taking off his shoes, Clem thought.

"Ho, hey" he called out, feeling foolish. "Sir? I brought in your books. I'm afraid they're probably a total loss." There was no reply. He felt absurdly that he was somehow in an empty shop yet, at the same time, as though he had dared interrupt some clandestine colloquy.

More, and worse, he feared that if he walked over, peered behind the counter, looked more closely, that that stringy, damp hair would be hanging from the gape-pored plastic head of a limp mannequin propped up against a row of gilded encyclopedias. But then the man grunted, and his head tilted slightly as he said something unintelligible, but identifiable as an acknowledgement. Good enough. Except that the muttering seemed to come from the speakers. Well, he probably had a microphone back there, for closing announcements and such.

Clem scanned the sun-faded books along the shelves at the shelf below the window and noticed that, back across the street, the awning under which he'd been standing had given way and was waving crazily in the wind, a tattered black flag. Under that flag he saw a man standing. Slender, very tall, with horn rimmed glasses, arched brows, and a ball of gray hair at each ear. A smartly blocked black hat rested atop the man's head, and a pipe was clamped between his teeth at an aggressive angle. He seemed unaffected by the rain, unshaken by the wind. Clem thought the man was staring at him. Not one to shrink away, he returned the stare. The man did not react, just glared, in the pounding rain and the searing wind. Smoke streamed from his pipe in bursts as he sucked in and frogged out his hollow cheeks.

Clem turned, disturbed. The clerk still sat crouched behind his counter. It was hotter than hell, and Clem removed his overcoat. He folded it and lay it over the arm of a frayed easy chair on which a tower of art books leaned. He loosened his tie and rolled up his shirtsleeves. Then, from the sound of it, the air conditioning kicked in, but Clem felt no relief, no welcome rush of cool air. He turned...it was not the AC after all; the rain had somehow gotten stronger, seething, roaring, blurring everything outside. Thunder stuttered and chuckled. Across the street the old man stood firm in the downpour, a blurred black line under a whipping black flag. Clem turned and walked deeper into the store. An odor like a damp attic, like wet papers, permeated everything. He saw a map that indicated the location of books, and noted that there was a local history section.

He swiftly navigated the maze of towering shelves until he found the alcove in question, but blocking the shelves

was a tall and bow-backed woman in a damp, limp blouse
that hung just above her bare knees. She was dragging a dry
finger across the spines of the books as though playing a
giant harp. Clem noted red cracks in the flesh of that finger.
Her head, slathered in flat, colorless hair, tilted like that of a
curious dog. She was barefoot, pale and pink. Her
unpainted toes drummed the carpet. Clem saw then that
the back of her neck was patterned in diamond-shaped red
welts, as though she'd been pushed against a chain link
fence. He harrumphed and did a bit of a pantomime of
trying to lean around her or look past her, but she seemed
oblivious. Feeling irritation and a touch of unease, he
turned and walked toward the door.

But, wait. Across from the register there were stairs
leading down to a sub-level. He walked over, and tacked to
the molding was a laminated sign that indicated many more
sections, including, he noted, a section called Local Lore and
Legend. There, he thought, he might find a book or two
that might flesh out the scant material in the dossier, or at
least focus his search for the group behind the illicit radio
station. He descended. When he reached the bottom he
saw that the bookshelves extended far beyond the
upstairs...below the adjacent pharmacy, certainly, and, I'll be
damned, well beyond even that. Thinking on it, Clem
surmised that the narrow basement, whose shelves were set

up as to make two long corridors lined with books, went past the parameters of the building as well. A crudely drawn map on the wall indicated the categories. The section he sought seemed to be, of course, at the farthest point. He headed in that direction. He noted along the way an area with an oval rug ringed with easy chairs and old rusted tray tables. In one of the chairs, a long haired black cat snored nasally. It shifted its weight when Clem walked by, raising its head sufficiently to reveal a watchful, if cataracted, yellow eye.

A few paces along, a book in the prodigious Occult section caught Clem's eye. It was tall, nearly reaching up to his hip, wedged in among dwarfed, moldy hardbacks, some green with biopredation. Abrecan Geist, read the name stretched along the spine in a jagged scrawl. The cover was devoid of art or word, but was a golden color, very finely tessellated, and intermittently tarnished with elongated brownish spots. The moment he grabbed the book to dislodge it, he felt it somehow contract. As he watched, wide-eyed, the whole surface of the book horripilated and flushed red. He flung it to the floor in disgust and horror. The cat started, wide-eyed, then put one paw over the other and set down his chin to resume his sleep.

Let's get the hell out of here, Clem thought. Around the cat, up the stairs, past the clerk who, let's face facts, is a propped up corpse, avoiding the thin woman, out the door, dodging the ancient creep under the awning. Let's get drenched, but let's get to the car, and drive straight to DC, leaving the clothes and that damned dossier and these doomed and haunted towns forever.

He stopped. Breathed. He was on the clock, and that horrid book was clearly planted there to throw him off the trail. It's effects, he thought madly. Special...special effects. He left the book on the floor and continued toward the dimly lit reaches of the basement. He reached the end where books were piled sufficiently high to block the lower shelves. Others were fanned across the floors. The books here seemed to consist mainly of European history and pictorials. He looked vainly for a local section, and then saw that the wall was not, in fact, a wall, but a densely packed shelf behind which another set of stairs descended into darkness. There was no "NO ADMITTANCE" sign, no chain, so Clem felt along the wall and then above his head until he found a string. He pulled it and saw a faint orange glow from somewhere below.

Nowhere to go but down, he thought, and descended. The stairs were narrow, grazing his shoulders on both sides.

The lowest room was not much bigger than a walk-in closet. There were two waist-high bookcases and a sagging loveseat between them. What little light there was glowed from recessed lights in the prodigiously cobwebbed stone ceiling. One of the bookcases seemed to consist of books, many disbound or slant-spined, by local poets and authors; the other shelf was the one he sought. He did notice on the lowest shelf of the former a fat, mouldering old tome bearing the name Abrecan Geist, but the binding proved nothing more than buckram, and the pages were yellowed and fragile, rendering the text and illustrations quite impossible to read. Turning back to the Local Lore section, he noted among whip-stitched chapbooks a thick tome entitled "Western Massachusetts Witch-Cults and Covens," authored by a Rangel Bantam. He plucked it out and fell backward into the loveseat.

The frontispiece was a photograph of a group of men congregated on stone steps familiar to him as those of Northampton's City Hall, a building that looked to him like some kind of boxy medieval castle, complete with balistraria and Norman towers. The men were gravely countenanced and pit-eyed, affecting postures of arrogant defiance. All wore smirks suggesting shared secrets. They were dressed in formal topcoats. Several men wore top-hats; two sported monocles. Tiered surnames in script at their feet identified the men above: Whiteshirt, Slaughton, Gare, Dither. Morphew, Lusk, Stockton, Ronstadt, Geist. Geist! The author of that horrible skin-bound book was a bald, stout man whose cheeks were stippled with acne scars. He wore a patterned ascot and a vest.

The other figure that struck him was that of Stockton. Taller than the other men, and positioned prominently, his face was lined, brows thick and furrowed, lips thin. Angled across his torso was a walking stick with a cat's head grip. The fingers clasping the walking stick were long, almost feminine, each encircled with several rings forged in the shapes of mystical symbols. There was something in the man's eyes...it seemed as though the man in the picture was looking across time up from the book at Clem, challenging, cajoling...glaring. In a familiar way. His jaw hanging, his eyes wide, Clem flipped to the table of contents: An Incident in Southwick, The Monson Magicians, The Warlock of Williamsburg, The Magi of the Second Laugh, Anna Gare and The Hilltown Ten.

The name pecked at his brain. Gare. The name of the store. He flipped back to the picture. He had missed her the first time: among the men, mostly obscured, stood a thin woman in petticoats: Anne Gare. Her hair was slack, one of her bony hands resting on the shoulder of Stockton. A flaw in the printing or in the photography distorted her features, though--her lower face appeared bulged, lips almost a perfect circle topped by an upcurved, flattened nose and slits for eyes.

Clem realized that he had been, for the last few moments, hearing a dribbling sound, a low and burbling trickle. He placed the book down on the cushion next to him and stood. As he approached the stairs, he saw that a thin stream of water was dribbling down the steps and puddling in the cracks and crevices in the concrete floor. It smelled dank, brackish. Then, suddenly, the entire stairway was flooded with bright light. Wincing, Clem squinted, hand at his brow, up the stairs. They were wet and reflected the light back at him. He could make out a thin black, jagged shadow culminating three steps from the floor in the shape of an elongated jutting pipe and an upside down hat. He looked at the top of the stairs, but all he could see was a slender silhouette framed in blinding light. "There's a HOLE in the BUCKET," it sang out in a gurgling, insinuating voice, "Dear LIZA, dear LIZA."

Clem knew what was coming next, but before he could turn, a high-pitched bubbling voice gurgled directly behind him. "Well FIX it, dear HENRY, dear HENRY, dear HENRY!"

Clem wheeled around and fell back against the stairs. It was the thin woman from the Local History section--it was Anne Gare. He now knew there had been no flaw in the printing, no flaw in the photograph. She opened her mouth as if to speak, revealing wide, flat yellow teeth, and then her jaw appeared to unhinge, her chin falling slack against her chest. Water poured from her grotesque mouth in a reeking rush, and behind Clem more water poured down the stairs in seething, stinking, roiling waves. The foul, bubbling water engulfed Clem and engulfed Anne Gare, in an instant filling the small room and climbing the stairs like a living thing. Clem was pulled from his feet. He held his breath for as long as he could. Then he let go, wrenching open his mouth in the vain lust for air, and the water filled his throat and lungs like a fist opening inside his chest. His body wrenched once, twice, then hung limply, bubbles rising from his slack mouth.

In the cloudy water, in the rippling bluish lamplight, Clem and Anne Gare danced a slow and majestic dance, her blouse twirling languidly at her thighs, his overcoat forming a cape that fluttered dreamily above him. Floating, floating, they circled each other among the books that rose from the floor and the shelves and fluttered about them like winged things.

the ballad of nathan whiteshirt

NATHAN WHITESHIRT remained unmarried for the whole of his fifty years. He lived in a two story house with a detectable tilt. Cats were frequently seen in the windows. He kept an unknown number.

NATHAN WHITESHIRT was thin, tall but stooped, his eyes bold and colorless under long, low brows. He was often the subject of rumors, particularly, but not exclusively, among the children of the town.

William Chesterfield, 8, claimed he saw NATHAN WHITESHIRT sitting high in a treetop, weeping.

Cynthia Blamefoot, 10, said she hears NATHAN WHITESHIRT singing obscene songs outside her window at night.

Robert Rutherford, 11, said that he saw NATHAN WHITESHIRT attack a dog and bite into its belly until a great flood of blood sprayed forth.

Michael Stark, 38, swears he saw NATHAN WHITESHIRT climb the venerable churchtower like a nimble spider.

Richard Wren, 72, won't speak aloud the name of NATHAN WHITESHIRT for fear NATHAN WHITESHIRT will murder his wife.

Stanley N. Toothburgle, 89, claims that NATHAN WHITESHIRT humiliates him by pulling obscenely at his pajamas when he makes his slow and painful way down the long hall for a piss at night.

It was rumored that before Winnifred Williston was found deceased in her bathroom, she had seen NATHAN WHITESHIRT when she pulled back the curtain to enter the bath.

When Father Ezekiel Shineface murdered a parishioner with whom it was rumored he was having an affair, some said that he had caught NATHAN WHITESHIRT and she engaged in an act of execrable obscenity in the confessional.

accident

"Look at the dead girl," Marie said, or that's what I *thought* she said. I replied--mm'hm--and the moment was past.

We were eating at Webster's and the girl and her parents were in the booth across from ours or, rather, the parents were in the booth. The girl, maybe nine or ten, was twirling in the aisle like a ballerina. "Look, mom," she kept saying. "Look!"

The parents didn't spare her so much as a glance. They looked haggard, and ate in silence. The man, balding and pale, had a look of concentration on his face. He ate voraciously and noisily, but betrayed no enjoyment. The woman was plain, her hair crowded into her face. She winced at the girl's entreaties, but otherwise looked as blank as the grille of a car.

I looked again at the girl, trying not to stare openly. I wondered if I hadn't misheard Marie. The girl looked wispy and somehow transparent, like a moth whose wings have been rubbed free of dust. She was so pale as to seem almost translucent, but betraying on her arms intricate webs of pale blue veins. There were dark circles around the girl's eyes, most times obscured by ringlets of hair so blond it looked almost white. Her hands were bony and looked fragile.

"She's a little sparkplug," Marie whispered. I'm sure that's what she whispered.

Suddenly there was a burst of static from the restaurant's speakers, which 'till then had been playing some local station too low to hear. The lights in the restaurant brightened, the girl spun madly in the aisle, and a thrumming surf music riff seemed to pass from the back of the dining room, over our table, to the front. A loud, low voice murmured something unintelligible, shaking the plates and glassware on the tables.

Then the power went out. Once my eyes adjusted, I could see everything fairly well, thanks to the streetlights, which were still on. People at their tables were looking around. Some stood and looked at the windows towards the shadowy turnpike. The family across from us continued to eat, as though nothing had happened. But now the girl was seated with them, staring agape at her plate, where a breaded king crab floated in a miasma of oil like a crusted bug in a long abandoned wading pool.

a world of lucretias and ledas

In a copse of trees near the river a young girl plays with a grey, exsanguined doll, bending its arms and balling its hands into fists. The doll's head hangs limp, a swollen purple tongue protruding from between black lips.

In the river is a man on a boat. The boat bobs in the water. The man can hear the sounds of the water lapping on the shore. The sun hangs high in the sky, enveloped in morning haze. A bird screeches. The man sits, hugging his knees, shivering. His breaths come in rasps. Suddenly he stands and steps silently off of the boat, slipping like a knife into the water. The ripples rock the boat slightly, then fade. The surface is again still. The boat drifts slowly towards shore.

I am standing on the banks of the river in my topcoat, leaning heavily on my cane, acorns and incarnadine leaves falling around me like rain. My kerchief, stuffed into my side pocket, is soaked with saliva and vomitus. I can feel it through the fabric. My shoes are caked in red mud. Somewhere behind me the town is waking, people wandering out onto the streets, shopkeepers uncloaking displays and unlatching doors. Somewhere, a woman is screaming as she runs barefoot through shattered glass to an empty crib.

I had awakened early, in darkness, my cat Leopold stretched across my stomach. I shoved him aside, went into the bathroom to evacuate my bowels. My stools were deep black and long, like spears. I dressed by lamplight and walked out onto Elm St. The sky was black. As I walked through and past the town, the sky went a deep blue that signaled the coming of dawn. There were clouds though, long and black and pointed. The clouds looked like murder.

This has been Jebediah Blackstye with the WXXT traffic report. Up next, Ben Stockton with the weather. WXXT, the Valley's only Real Radio.

cat-tails and rushes

In 1818 a fire tore through St. Feuster's Nursery on Elm Street in Northampton, Massachusetts. A cook in the kitchen had been seized by fits, and had flung a lit wooden match into a pile of soiled aprons. The nursery had housed 32 baby boys and girls, watched over by a staff of nine. Strangely, the women who fled saved all the girls; no men or boys survived, at least not in the recognized sense of the word.

I was part of a crew charged with cleaning the site. Armed with sledgehammers, pickaxes, shovels, buckets, chemicals and solvents, we resolved to destroy or remove all that remained, leaving only the stone cellar, scorched, but, it was hoped, salvageable. After three days we had cleared what remained of the walls and ruined floors from ground level, and had in front of us the recovery of the bodies from the rubble in the hole that remained.

The work was difficult, the task strenuous and grim. I was regularly short with my wife and my boy, and I slept fitfully. In some stretches of sleep I'd dream. In one dream a wooden box with a rusted metal grate told me in a slurred voice that I could count on nothing. Then worms poured through the grate like living liquid. I tried to flee, and it was as though I were running through water. In another dream angels hovered among leafless treetops at dusk. I watched from a hammock made of muscle and sinew which swung dreamily over an expanse of smoldering ash. I saw that the angels bore the rotting faces of dead goats, their toothy mouths ringed with green mucous. One hovered almost above me, head lolling heavily. Horribly, I could see up its gossamer frock; past its twisted-toed feet and knotted, gnarled legs; up to its abominable sex. What I saw I will not describe, but it filled me with panic, horror, and hopelessness.

The morning it happened was grey and cold and humid. Roderick Whittier, who had been sweeping ash from atop cabinets, scrambled up the blackened, tumbled bricks, cracking his fingernails, shrieking and cursing. Something had moved in the ash. I looked and a baby blackened like seared meat emerged from the wreckage. Brilliant blue eyes opened in the blackness of the ruined face. They seemed possessed of a knowledge, or an intelligence, that was impossible. Its tiny hands raised and it began peeling from its head blackened strips of burnt flesh, as blood poured down its visage. It did not cry. It did not make a sound. It only stared.

Whittier, an obstinate, thick dud of a man, began frantically reciting a fractured version of the Lord's Prayer:

Our Father

Who aren't in Heaven

Hollow be thy name

Thy kingdom done…

I held up a hand and he stopped, but began gulping rapidly. I could only stand stunned, and a nurse who had been watching from the treeline bolted forward and plunged down into the cellar. She grabbed the baby and helped it pull at its stinking black rind. She was sobbing, and her eyes were red. I accompanied her to the offices of my family doctor, the venerable Dr. Gladmost Alespiller. He took in the infant, and set up a room for him in a nursery that had been meant for his own son, who had died in childbirth, dragging Mrs. Alespiller with him back into blackness.

The nurse took up residence with the young doctor. It was quite a scandalous arrangement for the time, an abominable coupling with an abomination for a child. They seldom left the house, and not long after, the good Doctor stopped seeing patients. Walking by at night became a hobby for the curious. Sometimes the sounds of the couple's lovemaking could be discerned, and it was all shrieks and curses and mutterings. The next window over was that of the nursery. It glowed warmly, as though beckoning to cold travelers. No one knew what happened to the boy until much later, of course.

the first to die

On 12 November 1923, an overcast, drizzling day, the Bridge Street Cemetery was empty of living souls, save an elderly couple visiting the grave of their daughter, the victim of a ghastly murder as yet unsolved. At length they rose carefully from their knees, clasped swollen, liver spotted hands, and walked the grounds at a snail's pace, shoulder to shoulder, heads down.

As they passed a large mausoleum, the old man heard a crack, as that of an aged planck of wood being forcefully split. His companion heard nothing. As they rounded the curve on the walk, he spied a thin tombstone split down the middle in a cloud of dissolved stone. Then suddenly, shockingly, a splintered and bowed oak coffin launched forth from the earth like a rocket, in an explosion of sodden dirt and rocks and roots. For a moment it seemed to hang in the grey sky, then it landed hard acrost a wrought iron gate, spilling its grim contents heavily onto the wet ground.

The body, thirteen weeks under, was trembling with the crude and squirming purple denizens of the deep ground. Grey flesh clung to and hung from the dirty bone of the collapsed face. Incredibly, the thing clasped at the top of the gate and pulled itself to a crouching position.

It then began taking horrific, shambling, shaking steps in the direction of the stunned elders, each step shaking loose showers of dirt and beetles from its torn suit. Its jaw hung open obscenely, busted at its leftward hinge and bouncing brokenly as the thing lurched and pulled and limped forward.

And as I neared them, they at once turned and broke into a miserable parody of a run, the woman emitting, "Oh...oh...oh..." I laughed and it sounded like rocks pushing insistently against a shit-covered wall. As I approached the fleeing couple my femur cracked wetly and I tumbled to one knee, which broke loose at the hinge and splayed me out across a flat grave marker. I began dragging myself still forward. I found another fence and pulled myself up as the car shuttled away the mortified seniors, its engine attempting to roar but mostly belching and farting out rancid grey clouds. Thus thwarted, I turned...

...to find four venerable and familiar men standing in a half circle before me. "Benjamin," I said, my dry tongue pushing upward through black mud. "Be still," said Guy and pulled from his vestments a thick volume with a cracked spine and water bloated brown pages. The men, my friends, spoke in unison in an unfamiliar tongue. At length I felt myself crumple and fall, and yet I still stood. I looked down upon my shattered, rotted remains as though they were foul robes dropped at my feet at the commencement of some dark orgy. I looked back up at my companions, my saviors.

Minutes later, sauntering downtown, we came upon a motorcar on its side, its wheels spinning vainly. The old man from the cemetery was pulling himself from the wreck through a fetid stew of his wife's shredded bowels and broken glass and a lake of blood. We gathered around him and tore him to pieces. Benjamin was cackling and it shot fear through me and shutters and blinds closed and horses reared and the ghostly sun took shelter in an ancient elm and my throat was full of blood and dogs barked like an insane chorus and I was home and new born and ready to fuck.

the gossip hour

In early 1904 rumors began circling in the taverns and restaurants of an increase in occult dabblings amongst certain town officials in collusion with the strange and silent men sometimes seen gathering on corners and in parks and schoolyards. Unconfirmed reports of inexplicable happenings circulated in the sewing circles and poker games and barber shops.

There was the story of the Whately baby born with gossamer black wings that grew from its shoulder blades and folded intricately behind its tiny pink back, and how the cursed thing, brought to the church to be blessed and cleansed of sin, flew up into the rafters and micturated blood upon the altar and the preacher and the congregation...

...and of the house which, when chopped with an axe, sprayed forth a fountain of blood...

...and of the boy with the head of a pig seen digging furiously at the ground in cemeteries or snorting madly at passing carriages...

...and of the child of but two who murdered her parents and chewed out their throats...

...and of the double headed worms burrowed into bread and uncooked meats that poisoned and made madmen out of several Hatfield townsfolk...

...and of the beetles the size of dinner plates that attached to the heads of unfortunate patients of the Northampton Lunatic Hospital, collapsing their skulls and liquefying their tortured brains.

The Gazette's reporters tried to provide logical explanations for the disturbances and rumors thereof, but the wild talk continued unabated, as wild talk might in a small New England town nestled by a restless river.

sermon

Brothers and sisters, the Lord God has left me in silence. My calls for His words and guidance echo back to me in this hollow cave with its tuneless organ, its cracked and colored windows, its inhospitably tilted pews. I seek His throne and find it empty save for splinters. I seek His eyes and they are milky with cataracts. I reach for His hand and it crumples in mine like rotten fruit. I seek His footprints and they fill with black blood.

The Lord, in a word, has stopped speaking to me.

The rectory is cold and dank, my sermons degenerate into gibberish, and His rod and His staff skewer me, fixing me to the ground in this colorless land of wheeled and windowed tombs.

And so I turn to you, my weary congregation, meek and humble, your Sunday best not quite good enough, with holes in your shoes and in your suits, your fabrics alive with flies, your buttons askew, your tongues swollen to black and bursting. I implore you to raise your cracked voices to the Lord and beg His return. The microphones are open and we are on the air. Clear your throats of beetles, of mud and decay, and open up your hymnals to page 40-12. Our listening audience awaits. Be sure to project.

the reddening dusk

In the high heat of August I hobbled along the secluded path which veined through the reedy meadows, through the bluets and the crabgrass, farther and farther from the clamor of downtown, to The House. A big black bird tittered in a barren tree. My bad leg thrummed and throbbed in rhythm with my bad teeth, jolting me to twitches.

Still I propelled myself forward, for my Master had promised that he would bring forth from the grave my sweet Sylvia, whole and upright and real, so that I might finally have her for my own, in The House, Alone and No One Else.

My Sylvia! Her eyes, impossibly green! Her softness and pink fat! Her bonnet and her dress and its flounces! Her secret parts a hidden pond in which I swum majestic and free! Her mouth, so small, but so shrill! Her hands, which did thrice betray me but did then stroke me until I could only forgive! Her eyes again, in terror and each reflecting my livid visage and the glint of my knife! My sorrow! My sorrow!

GONE THESE MANY YEARS, I bellowed, and the cicadas kicked up a creaky chorus!

BACK TO ME FOREVER, I cried, and a cloud of birds shot up through the treetops bleating!

FORGIVE ME SHE WILL AND FOLD IN MY EMBRACE, I hollered, and the moon fair swung in the sky like a watch on a chain!

HAPPY DAYS AND...

"Shaddap!"

I stopped cold. Who was out here in this waning hot afternoon, this reddening dusk?

"Shaddap and get in the house!"

The House! I now saw through the wall of trees the yellow rectangles flickering like candles. I pushed through the underbrush. It tore at my clothes, poked through my ribs, scratched around my eyes and tore at my trousers. Things inside me pulled and broke, bright white pains galloped through my joints, hot knives pinwheeled through my guts, but I pushed my way past the trees and through the crooked door into a cold foyer of dark wood and cobwebbed chairs.

And now, down the stairs came my master, arms aloft, as though an angel descending in a ray of sunlight. So young, I thought. So young and cruel-eyed. A wispy halo of yellow hair and a lipless scar for a mouth.

"Fuck you yelling about?" my master sang and I bowed in supplication. But then my elation, my anticipation, turned

143

into terror. What if my master had failed me? What if my Sylvia did not await me, as promised, in this Hidden House?

My master regarded me with a slack mouth and eyeballs like blue yolks. "LOOK at you!", he whispered. And, "Guys!", he yelled, and two young men, whip-thin and long of hair emerged from a doorway to my right. One of them looked at me and shrieked. The other picked up a small round table and jabbed it in my direction, the cobwebs tickling at my face with each thrust. The boy's breathing was ragged, his moon-face white and weathered.

"Goddammit," I croaked. "WHERE IS MY SYLVIA?" And my master's minions rushed at and then around me, the one boy jabbing the table at me, creasing my skull. I went to my knees and saw blood dash onto the floorboards...but, no. Not blood. A spray of dirt, in which fat pink worms writhed like limbless pigs. Before I could make sense of this, the table walloped me again and I heard the boys break through the door and struggle through the underbrush, shrieking and weeping.

My master now stood over me. "In the side room," he said, and fled after his friends. I rose, with some difficulty, and went into the room from whence the boys had come. A couch, bowed and faded, its flower pattern barely discernible under a blanket of dust. A flat, low table with an ashtray piled over with ash...so much ash...grey and piled and spilling over the edge...and reaching up through the ash a diamond ring and a painted fingernail. My Sylvia.

I hoofed it out the door, sobbing and gibbering and bellowing.

GONE TO ME FOREVER, I cried, and a whimper came from somewhere!

WAKED AND BETRAYED AND BEATEN, I bellowed, and my master lay beneath me with purple ankle and foot set wrong!

AND ALONE AND ALONE AND ALONE, I hollered, and I opened my master's belly and did crawl inside as the night crashed down and the trees screamed!